THE FAMOUS FIVE IN DEADLY DANGER

THE FAMOUS FIVE are Julian, Dick, George, (Georgina by rights), Anne and Timmy the dog.

A West Indian island, complete with volcano and poisonous snakes, is the dangerously exciting setting for the Famous Five's Easter holiday. And staying with a famous scientist there, the Five quickly find themselves plunged into adventure. It seems their host is under threat from a rival – an evil 'doctor' who will do anything to lay his hands on the valuable results of the scientist's research. The Five decide to lend a hand and soon find themselves tackling a most deadly enemy . . .

Also available from Knight Books

The Famous Five in Deadly Danger

A new adventure of the
characters created by
Enid Blyton, told by Claude
Voilier, translated by
Anthea Bell

Illustrated by Bob Harvey

KNIGHT BOOKS
Hodder and Stoughton

Copyright © Librairie Hachette 1978

First published in France as Les Cinq aux Rendez-vous du Diable

English language translation copyright © Hodder & Stoughton Ltd. 1986

Illustrations copyright © Hodder & Stoughton Ltd. 1986

First published in Great Britain by Knight Books 1986
Fifth impression 1988

British Library C.I.P.

Voilier, Claude
    The Famous Five in deadly danger: a new adventure of the characters created by Enid Blyton.
    I. Title   II. Harvey, Bob
    III. Le cinq aux rendezvous du Diable. *English*
    843'.914[J]   PZ7

ISBN 0-340-37842-5

Printed and bound in Great Britain for Hodder and Stoughton Paperbacks, a division of Hodder and Stoughton Ltd., Mill Road, Dunton Green, Sevenoaks, Kent TN13 2YA (Editorial Office: 47 Bedford Square, London WC1B 3DP) by Richard Clay Ltd., Bungay, Suffolk.

CONTENTS

Chapter One

OFF TO MARTINIQUE

George, Julian, Dick and Anne heard the air hostess's voice coming over the loudspeaker: 'Ladies and gentlemen, please put out your cigarettes and fasten your seat-belts. We are now flying over the coast of Martinique, and we shall be coming down at Lamentin International Airport in a few minutes' time.'

The big aircraft had left London that morning, and now it had reached the Windward Islands.

'At last!' said George. 'Eight hours' flying is quite enough for me, and it must have been *more* than enough for poor old Timmy. I can't wait to see him again – I do wish they didn't make him travel with the baggage! He'll be ravenous for his supper now, too.'

Dick's nose was glued to the porthole as he looked down at the beautiful green island with its white beaches, over which they were flying.

'Supper?' he said, laughing. 'You've forgotten about time zones, George! We may have been flying for eight hours, but it's still only about three in the afternoon in Martinique!'

'Yes, and how's Timmy to know that?' said George indignantly. 'He'll still be hungry, won't he?'

Julian and Anne were craning their necks to see the island too.

'Here we are,' said Julian. 'Just coming down now!'

They felt the shudder of landing and the plane taxied a short distance along the runway before coming to a halt.

What an exciting moment! Uncle Quentin, George's father, who was famous all over the world for his important scientific work, had been invited to go to a big scientists' conference in the West Indian island of Martinique – and the children had been thrilled to hear that he intended to take them and Aunt Fanny with him. George and her cousins had all done well at school last term, and Uncle Quentin thought it would be a good reward to take them to the West Indies for their Easter holidays.

'You're sure to find it educational,' he told them. 'You'll be able to see something of the island, and learn a great many interesting things. We are going to stay with my old friend and colleague, Dr Paul Anderson. He has a large villa on the coast near a little fishing town called Tartane. He and his wife insisted on asking us all to stay – including Timmy!'

'As if I'd go without him!' said George. 'Dear old Tim!'

As far as the children could see, there was only one drawback – most of the people of Martinique, Uncle Quentin told them, spoke French. 'Well, I don't mind practising mine,' said Julian. 'I was rather enjoying the French lessons at school last term.'

'You may find that West Indian French doesn't sound quite the same as what you've been taught,' Uncle Quentin said. 'A number of people speak what is called Creole – French with some African words mixed into it. But it won't do you any harm to try, my boy – I like to see you ready to work hard!' he added approvingly.

'Why does Dr Anderson live there instead of on one of the English-speaking islands?' Dick asked. 'If *I* lived in the West Indies, I'd want it to be somewhere they played cricket!'

'Well, for one thing my friend Anderson inherited his house on Martinique – it's been in his family a long while, and he didn't want to give it up. And there's another reason – to do with his work! I'll leave you to find out about that for yourselves,' said Uncle Quentin.

The children were rather intrigued.

'And your uncle has forgotten to tell you,' said Aunt Fanny, smiling, 'that all the people who work for Dr Anderson at his house, and in his scientific laboratory, come from the *British* West Indies, so you'll be able to understand them quite all right!'

'I'm sure you will get on well with the Andersons' son, too,' added Uncle Quentin. 'His name is Eric – he's nineteen, quite a lot older than any of you, but he has very kindly said he'd be happy to show you round.'

'Hurray!' the children had all shouted. 'Just think – we're going to the West Indies!'

And now here they were! Once they had collected their baggage, and of course Timmy, the children followed Uncle Quentin and Aunt Fanny through a crowd of cheerful people who were talking and laughing merrily. They stopped outside the airport building. The children saw beds of beautiful, brightly coloured flowers, and breathed in their fragrance.

'Anderson said he'd be sending someone to meet us,' said Uncle Quentin, looking slightly at a loss.

At that very moment, a tall, fair-haired young man came up to the travellers, smiling broadly. He had recognised them!

'You must be my father's friend Quentin Kirrin, sir!' the young man said, 'And Mrs Kirrin too!' He shook hands with Aunt Fanny and Uncle Quentin. 'I'm Eric Anderson,' he added. 'Sorry I'm late, but I had to go into Fort-de-France, the capital of this island, about something first – something that's rather a nuisance, but my father will tell you about it himself. Did you have a good journey? Come along this way, would you? The car's not far off.'

Eric had a pleasant, open face. The children liked him at first sight. He picked up Aunt Fanny's suitcase, and turned to them. 'And of course you're George, Julian, Dick and Anne.' George beamed at him. Why, he had even got her name right! She did hate to be called by her full, girl's name of Georgina, when she would so much rather have been a boy. 'As for Timmy,' Eric went on, 'he looks exactly like the photograph you sent us. He's – er – quite indescribable!'

'Woof!' Timmy agreed, realising that it was him Eric was talking about.

George wasn't absolutely sure that 'indescribable' was meant as a compliment, but she decided to take it as one.

'He's *better* than indescribable!' she said proudly. 'He's unique!'

And to his little mistress, Timmy really was the best and most beautiful dog in the whole world.

The Andersons' car was big and comfortable, and would easily take all of them. Eric drove for several kilometres on one of the good main roads leading away from the airport, and then turned right into a minor road.

'We're starting along the Caravelle peninsula now,' he told his passengers. 'It juts right out into the Atlantic, and it's a nature reserve. Our house, Hibiscus Villa, is just outside Tartane, about seven kilometres off, and my father's laboratory is five kilometres further on, on the very end of the peninsula. Look – you can see the sea to both right and left of you now!'

The scenery was really beautiful. George and her cousins were fascinated. 'I say, how lucky you are living on an island like this!' Julian said to Eric. 'What a splendid place!'

'I quite agree with you,' said Eric. 'And I'll take you to see all the sights of Martinique while you're here.'

Julian had more questions he would have liked to ask, but he had to wait because Uncle Quentin wanted to ask Eric about the work Dr Anderson was doing at the moment. Paul Anderson was a very famous scientist, and just now, as Uncle Quentin had told the children, he was doing research into the effects of the venom of pit-vipers, a kind of snake found in the West Indies and America. He hoped to find out how to use the venom to make medicinal drugs which could treat several serious kinds of illness.

Paul Anderson had inherited a family with his house, so he was a rich man. And because he was doing such valuable research work, a big scientific institute had given him a grant to build a laboratory. It was a very modern and well-equipped laboratory – Uncle Quentin had heard all about it from his friend, and couldn't wait to see it for himself. But when he asked Eric about his father's current research, the young man shook his head and looked rather worried.

'Father's not making much progress at the moment – he doesn't want to hurry things, of course, and unfortunately he's had some trouble recently,' he said.

'Trouble?' Dear me,' said Uncle Quentin. 'What kind of trouble?'

'Well, a couple of nights ago he discovered that someone had broken into his study at home and tried to force the safe where he keeps some of his secret formulae,' said Eric. 'In fact that's why I had to go into Fort-de-France just now, to ask if the police had got anywhere with their inquiries into the attempted burglary. Father has a friend who's a chief police Commissaire there. That's the equivalent of an English Superintendent,' he explained to the children. 'Well, here we are! He can tell you the rest of the story himself!'

The car drove in through the gates of a magnificent house, smothered in purple Bougainvillaea and the Hibiscus flowers that gave it its name. But George and her cousins were looking at each other, and not the flowers.

'What luck!' George couldn't help exclaiming. 'We've arrived right in the middle of a mystery!'

Hearing her, Eric smiled. 'I know what a reputation you Famous Five have for solving mysteries,' he said. 'Who knows – perhaps you can help with this one! But here's my mother to welcome you.'

As the visitors from England got out of the car, and a man helped Eric unload the suitcases, they saw a smiling woman come towards them.

'How nice to see you all!' Mrs Anderson told her guests. 'You must be tired and hungry after your long journey. Do come on to the veranda! Lilah is going to bring you something to eat and drink. And my husband should be back from his laboratory any moment now.'

Lilah, the Andersons' maid, was a pretty, brown-skinned woman. Smiling broadly at the children, she brought them a tray laden with good things to eat and drink. They specially enjoyed the delicious tropical fruits, and a cool drink which Lilah told them she made from guava juice.

Then Mrs Anderson showed her guests where they were going to sleep. The children had two rooms with a view of the sea, one room for George and Anne and one for the boys. They were delighted. However, they wouldn't see much more today, because the sun was already going down. The mountain rising behind Hibiscus Villa was casting purple shadows.

'The sun goes down about six o'clock here at all times of the year, summer and winter alike,' Eric told the children, 'and there's only a very brief period of twilight. You'll soon get used to it.'

Just then a small car drove up – it was Dr Anderson, who had left the family's bigger car for

Eric to take to the airport. He was delighted to see his friend Uncle Quentin and to welcome the whole family to his house.

'I hope you'll feel quite at home here,' he told them. 'And I'll take you to see my laboratory tomorrow, Quentin, old fellow.' Then the smile faded from his face.

Dick was dying to ask questions about the burglary, and at this point he couldn't help joining in the grown-ups' conversation. 'I say, sir — Eric told us what happened the other day. About somebody trying to burgle your study!'

Dr Anderson looked at the children in some surprise at first, but then he smiled again.

'I'd quite forgotten what gluttons for mystery you are!' he said. 'But Quentin has often written to me about your adventures. Young as you are, I hear you've solved a good many strange cases. Some that have even baffled the police, so your father tells me, George!'

'Well — we *have* been lucky sometimes, sir,' said Julian modestly.

'George and my brothers are awfully clever,' Anne told Dr Anderson.

'And you're no fool either, Anne!' George told her cousin. 'Don't forget good old Timmy, either! He's a wonderful sleuth-hound.'

That made Dr Anderson laugh. 'Unfortunately, there isn't any mystery here,' he told the children. 'I already know who was responsible.'

George looked disappointed. 'Oh,' she said. 'You mean you know who broke into your house?'

'I'm more or less certain – but officially I can't do anything except tell the police my suspicions. I can't make any accusations, because I have no proof to offer. So I've had to be content with reporting a case of breaking and entering.'

'Tell us about it, Paul, will you?' said Uncle Quentin. 'That is, if you don't mind letting us know the full story.'

'Oh, not in the least,' said Dr Anderson. 'It was like this . . .'

Chapter Two

AT THE LABORATORY

'I keep most of the formulae of my discoveries in a safe at the laboratory,' Dr Anderson told his guests. 'However, I take the ones I'm working on at the moment everywhere with me. And the day before yesterday I brought some formulae home in the evening. I worked on them after supper, and then I locked them in the wall-safe in my study before I went to bed. First thing yesterday morning, Lilah was horrified to find a broken window. Somebody had climbed over the garden railings in the night and broken into the villa. And there were marks on the safe showing that an attempt had been made to open it – but an unsuccessful one, I'm glad to say. The safe is set firmly into the wall, and its contents are well protected. The burglar would have had to use a hammer and chisel to get it out, and that would have taken a long time and made a lot of noise, rousing the whole household!'

'So he left empty-handed?' asked Julian.

'Yes, but I very much fear he will return to the attack! Either here, or at the laboratory.'

'You were saying just now that you suspected someone,' Uncle Quentin reminded his friend.

'Well, yes, I do,' said Dr Anderson. 'There are a good many research laboratories in different countries that would be very glad to have the results of my work, but I believe I have only one really dangerous rival. And that's a man living on this very island called Dr Stein – nobody knows just what his nationality is, but he's a very slippery fish indeed, and with a reputation for shady dealing. I'm afraid he's capable of anything.'

George, Julian, Dick and Anne pricked up their ears. There might not be any actual mystery to solve, but perhaps they could at least help Dr Anderson in some way. They felt sure they could stand up to this Dr Stein.

'When you say Dr Stein's capable of anything, you mean he might steal your formulae?' asked Anne. 'I suppose they must be very important and very valuable.'

Dr Anderson smiled at the little girl. 'Yes, they are! I'm nowhere near the end of my work yet, but my research is getting along very well indeed. I'm sure I'm on the right track. My rivals would very much like to get hold of my formulae, even at their present stage. However, if anyone actually tried using the medicinal drugs I'm developing just as they are now, before they've been fully tested and their composition properly worked out, they might do more harm than good, especially in the hands of the kind of unscrupulous people who put their own interests before the health of the sick people whom I hope my work will help.'

It all sounded very interesting – but the children suddenly realised that they were feeling extremely tired, after such a long and exciting day. They went to bed quite early, and slept soundly all night long. When George woke next morning, the sun was streaming into her bedroom.

'Wake up, Anne!' she called. 'Time to get up!'

Anne opened her eyes, smiled at her cousin and jumped out of bed. Not long afterwards the Five were all down in the dining room, where Eric was waiting for them. Lilah came in, smiling, with a most unusual breakfast: guava juice, fresh pineapple, coffee, buttered toast and papaya jam. It was delicious.

'Your father and mine have gone off to the laboratory, deep in scientific talk,' Eric told the children. 'And our mothers have gone shopping. I suggest we go out ourselves when you've finished breakfast.'

'Woof!' said Timmy. He liked the idea of going out.

'I have a small car of my own,' Eric went on. 'Father gave it to me for my nineteenth birthday. It'll be a bit of a squash, but I think we can all get in it, and as I'm on vacation from college at the moment, my time's my own, so I can show you round the island.'

'What are you going to do when you've finished studying, Eric?' Dick asked their new friend.

'I mean to go in for scientific research, like my father,' Eric said.

'I say,' George suddenly asked, 'can you tell us any more about that Dr Stein your father mentioned last night?'

'Dr Stein? Oh yes! He had the cheek to ask Father either to sell him his formulae or to go into partnership with him. Father sent him off with a flea in his ear, I can tell you! Stein is a thoroughly unscrupulous man. I suspect he hasn't got any real right even to call himself *doctor*. He thinks of nothing but the commercial value of scientific research, and how much money could be made out of Father's discoveries.'

'Then Dr Anderson really thinks it was Dr Stein who tried to burgle his safe?' asked Julian.

'He's sure of it! Nobody would have tried forcing the safe unless they were interested in the formulae. On an island like this, you see, everyone knows all about their neighbours, and it's common knowledge that my mother owns no valuable jewellery, and we settle our bills by cheque. So the only really valuable thing in Hibiscus Villa is the contents of the wall-safe in the study. And we believe that only Stein would have the nerve to try stealing them so boldly.'

'In fact, as long as he's on the loose, he's a threat to you,' George summed it up. 'Is that right?'

'Yes, I'm afraid it is,' Eric agreed. 'And yet we can't produce any concrete evidence against him, just as my father told you yesterday.'

'If only we could catch him red-handed!' said Dick.

'Well, maybe we *can*!' said George. Her eyes were shining with excitement. 'He'd better look out if he tries anything else!'

Eric smiled at her, but he shook his head. 'Don't be too hopeful,' he said. 'Stein is no fool! And he knows how to look after himself. He never goes anywhere without two bodyguards – one is a huge, strong man, and the other though not so impressive to look at, is as clever as a pocketful of monkeys! And Stein needs those bodyguards, because he has enemies. He's already swindled so many people that his victims would be happy to get their revenge on him.'

'Do you mean the police can't do anything about it?' asked Anne.

'Stein's cunning, you see – he keeps just within the law, or if he does break it, he makes sure that nothing can be proved against him,' Eric told her.

'I think this Dr Stein sounds rather interesting,' said George as if to herself, rising from the table. 'We could be in for an adventure . . .'

Eric fetched his little car, and asked the children

to get in. George and Timmy sat in the front with him, and Anne and the two boys squeezed into the back – at least little Anne didn't take up much space.

'I'd better warn you that the road's a bit bumpy from here to Devil's Point, at the end of the peninsula,' Eric told them, smiling. 'However, the scenery's good, and I'd like to show you my father's laboratory.'

It really was a beautiful road, As they drove along, Eric told the children about the places they were passing. Suddenly Anne let out an exclamation. 'Eric, what are those ruins down there?'

'Oh, that's Dubuch Castle,' Eric said. 'We'll visit it sometime – the place has quite a sinister reputation. It was a huge house really, not a real castle, and the owner used to keep his slaves in cells rather like dungeons. Look! We're nearly there now!'

In a moment Eric's little red car was driving along a concrete track which led to a white building with plate-glass windows shining in the sun.

'Devil's Point, and the laboratory!' he said. 'Right, then – here we are at our journey's end.' And he got out of the car.

The children got out too, and followed him into the building. It was a very handsome one. There was an entrance hall with a mosaic floor, and the atmosphere here was pleasantly cool. The hall was decorated with mirrors and tropical plants, and there was a little fountain of water splashing into its basin.

An old man came to meet them. He was dark-skinned and white-haired, and had a broad smile on his face as he greeted the new arrivals. 'Morning, Mr Eric!' he said cheerfully. 'And this little lady and the three young men here is come to stay, is they?'

George smiled happily back at the old man. He thought she really was the boy she looked like – and he wasn't the first to make that mistake! But she explained that she was really a girl, though she'd have preferred to be a boy, and the old man thought that was a very good joke and laughed heartily. Eric introduced them all.

'Victor has been with my father for years,' he told the children. 'He saw the laboratory built, and now he guards it day and night. He even insists on sleeping in the building, as a kind of night watch-man, which is very good of him indeed.'

'Why, that nothing, Mr Eric!' said the old man. 'Stand to reason I guard it for your Pa – he so good to me! He and his friend, they in the annexe this minute. You want to see the lab, eh?'

'Yes, that's right,' said Eric. 'Would you like to come with us and show my young friends round, Victor?'

Victor called a younger man to take his place in the entrance hall, and proudly showed Eric and the children into the main part of the building.

They had to go through a disinfection chamber first, as a precaution against disturbing any of the delicate experiments in the laboratory, and then they entered Dr Anderson's laboratory itself. It was the kind of modern building that any research scientist would love to have at his disposal, with several huge, well-aired and well-lit rooms, up-to-date equipment, and all sorts of top quality mineral and vegetable products for use as ingredients in various chemical preparations, plus a number of rats and guinea pigs on which Dr Anderson tested his new inventions.

Anne felt very sorry for the little creatures. 'Oh, poor things!' she said, looking at a cage full of guinea pigs. 'Aren't they sweet? I can't bear to think of them being used as laboratory animals, Eric.'

But Eric reassured the tender-hearted litle girl. 'My father is very human,' he said. 'He never, never does any vivisection, even under anaesthetic. He just tests the serums he develops on these little animals, and you must remember that it'll be thanks to them a great deal of life is saved.'

Julian was impressed by the sight of Dr Anderson's assistants at work in various parts of the laboratory building. The young research scientists were so absorbed in what they were doing that they hardly noticed the visitors at all. You could tell that they were fascinated by their work, Julian thought. No wonder Eric wanted to go in for scientific research too. It would be a great thing to help save human life.

'And here,' said Eric, opening another door, 'is the vivarium, where the snakes are kept!'

There was a sharp, pungent sort of smell in this room. Timmy growled quietly, looking a little frightened.

'Hush, Timmy!' said George, putting one hand on her dog's collar. 'There's nothing to be scared of – keep quiet, do.'

Victor was happy to introduce the children to 'his' snakes – he explained that he personally was in charge of them. There were several of them, enormous specimens, dozing in big glass cases which had stout wire netting over the top. The wire covers were firmly bolted in place. George was fascinated by the snakes – she had never seen anything like them before.

'Aren't they huge!' she said.

'They look pretty fierce,' Dick agreed.

Victor smiled. 'Oh yes, they terrible fierce!' he assured the children happily. 'They sleep all day, like now, but they very, very lively by night!'

The children wanted to know more about the snakes. 'Well, I won't bore you with too many technical details,' said Eric, 'but pit-vipers belong to the Crotalidae snake family, which includes rattlesnakes. There are two species here: their zoological names are *Bothrops atrox* and *Bothrops lanceolatus*. They can easily grow to as much as one

26

and three quarter or even two metres long. Cane-cutters at work in the sugar-cane fields have to be very careful if they meet one of these snakes – if they're bitten, they must have an injection of anti-snakebite serum as soon as possible, or they're sure to die.'

'Are the pit-vipers more dangerous than ordinary European vipers?' asked Julian.

'Yes, and they're even more dangerous than the African cobra. Their venom paralyses the victim's nervous centres and poisons his blood at the same time.'

'Ugh!' said Dick, shuddering. 'I hope there aren't many around on this island! We might meet one.'

'Don't worry,' said Eric. 'As Victor told you, they're nocturnal animals and don't come out until after sunset. And there are not as many on Martinique as there used to be. In other parts of the West Indies, they have almost died out – but my father needs them for his work.'

'He uses their venom in his experiments, doesn't he?' said George. 'So that's why he built the lab on this particular island! How on earth do you get the venom out of them, Eric?'

Just then a door opened behind her back, and Dr Anderson himself came into the room with Uncle Quentin.

'Ah, there you are, children!' said Dr Anderson. 'I thought Eric would bring you to see the lab. So you want to know how we extract the snake venom, do you, George? I'll show you.'

Watched by the fascinated children, he went over to one of the cases and unbolted its lid. He put one hand swiftly into the case and grabbed a snake just behind its head. Suddenly woken, the creature wriggled and writhed, trying to get away. But Victor had grasped the long, cylindrical body and was holding it in a firm grip. With his free hand, Dr Anderson picked up a little glass jar with a thin piece of paper covering its top.

'It's like a little jam-jar!' whispered Anne.

The scientist brought the pit-viper's head close to the jar and forced it to open its mouth. The furious reptile bit the first thing it could get at — its fangs went through the paper covering the jar, and its venom was caught inside the little glass container.

Dr Anderson and Victor put the snake back into its case. The watching children had turned a little pale.

'I say – isn't what you just did very dangerous, sir?' asked Julian.

'Well, we do have an accident now and then,' said Dr Anderson, 'but we always keep the antidote within reach. I was once bitten on the thumb, and Victor's been bitten three times. The third was a bad one, because it was only a month since he'd been bitten before.'

'We ready for anything.' said the old man,

smiling. 'We got plenty first-aid kits over here, all ready inject serum if we need.'

'Serum or no serum,' said George, shaking her head, 'I don't think *I'd* like to handle those snakes!'

'Woof, *woof*,' agreed Timmy, barking in a disgusted way. Everybody laughed.

'Well, time to go back to Hibiscus Villa,' said Dr Anderson. 'I just have to fetch something from my office here first.'

In his office, he showed Uncle Quentin and the children the huge steel safe where he kept the results of his research work.

'It's virtually impossible to force this safe,' he said, 'but one never knows – and with Dr Stein about, it seems I shall have to be on my guard.'

Chapter Three

DR STEIN

The two cars set off back down the road. The Five thought the island landscape looked even more beautiful than before in the bright mid-day sun.

'I suggest we go bathing this afternoon,' said Eric on the way back. 'We'll swim off the local beach – you'll find it's very nice in the water here, and there are no sharks about, which is one good thing about Martinique. It's not safe to bathe off many other West Indian islands, such as Jamaica, for instance, except in areas protected by netting.'

The children had a fine time swimming that afternoon, and next day Eric took them sight-seeing. Napoleon's wife, the Empress Josephine, he told them, had been born on Martinique, and they went to see her birthplace, which had an interesting little museum. On the way, the children admired the landscape of the southern part of the island. There were fields of sugar-cane, lush green trees, coconut palms and masses of flowers. When they had looked round the museum, Eric took them to another beach to bathe – this one was on the Caribbean shore of the island, and it was the first time they had ever bathed in such calm, clear sea-water. They spent a good hour swimming, playing in the sand, going back into the water for another swim, and running about in the sun to get dry.

'What a fine time we're having!' said Julian, as he got his clothes on again. 'I must say, it's jolly good of you to take us round Martinique like this, Eric! What's next on the programme?'

'Well, I thought we'd go to the capital, Fort-de-France, and have lunch in a nice little restaurant I know,' said Eric.

The Five thought the capital of the island was a very interesting place. There was a beautiful, big, green park, with a roofed-over market beside it. Dick stopped in front of a stall selling island crafts for souvenirs. He picked up a wide-brimmed hat, put it on and started fooling about. 'I think I'll keep it!' he said. 'Don't you think it suits me?' The lady selling the hats laughed at his antics and assured him that it suited him marvellously. Or so Eric told the children, translating her French which, just as Uncle Quentin had warned Julian, was a little hard to understand. She was still chuckling as she took the money for the hat. Then Timmy thought *he* would try a hat on too – he got his nose underneath a whole pile of them, and then lifted his head in the air. The pile toppled over, but there was still one broad-brimmed hat left on Timmy's head, half smothering him, and he couldn't see a thing. Suddenly panic-stricken, the poor dog went dashing about this way and that. He overturned a stall displaying shell necklaces, and another selling dolls in West Indian costume. Finally he backed towards a pool of fish, and fell in.

How everyone laughed! Luckily all the stall-holders were very good-natured people, and no harm had been done to any of their goods except the hat Timmy was wearing, which was a bit battered and wet by now. Julian, Dick, Anne and Eric could hardly do anything for laughing, and George, who had been chasing about after her dog, was quite out of breath. At last she was able to fish him out of the pool, and she decided she had better buy the hat!

'It will be fine once it's dried off,' she said, 'and I don't think Timmy will want to wear it again, somehow! So I can keep it for myself.'

'I think we could do with something nice and cool to drink after all that!' said Eric. 'The restaurant where I'm taking you is some way off, so let's go into this café.'

It was rather a smart café, full of people sipping drinks. The children sat at a table near the door and enjoyed tall, frosted glasses of iced pineapple juice. 'Funny how pineapple juice tastes so much better here than out of a tin at home,' said George contentedly.

As she sipped her juice, she glanced around her, and suddenly, at the far end of the room sitting at a table, she saw a thin, dark-haired white man talking in a low voice to two other men, who both had brown skins. One was very large and athletic-looking, and the other one was smaller. She would have thought no more of these three men if she hadn't happened to notice that the thin man kept giving Eric a nasty look. Rather intrigued, she told him in a whisper, 'Don't look round for a moment, but there's someone at the back of the café who seems very interested in you.'

'Is there?' said Eric, without turning his head.

'Yes – a thin man who seems to know you, and doesn't seem to like you much either!' said George. 'If looks could kill, I don't think you'd stand much chance.'

Anne had taken a quick look behind her. 'George is right,' she agreed. 'That man looks as nasty as one of those pit-vipers in the lab!'

Julian cautiously glanced round too. 'It's all right, you can look now, Eric,' he said. 'He's talking to one of his companions.'

So Eric turned round. 'Well, well!' he said quietly. 'Fancy meeting him here! Do you know who that man is?'

'I rather think I can guess,' said George. 'The big man is exactly my idea of a bodyguard – and

you told us Dr Stein always went about with two of them. *Is* it Dr Stein and his bodyguards?'

'It is indeed,' said Eric. 'Your guess is quite right, George. Well, it's not surprising if, as you say, that rascal doesn't seem to like me. After all, I'm my father's son, and everyone knows that he can't stand my father.'

'Those three look as if they were planning something nasty,' said Julian, frowning.

'More than likely!' Eric told him. 'I dare say Stein is still angry that he failed to burgle the safe at Hibiscus Villa. I wouldn't be at all surprised if he didn't make another attempt to injure my father soon, in one way or another.'

Eric sounded quite calm, but the children could tell he was worried, all the same. Dick leaned forward. 'I say, Eric, you know you can count on us, don't you?' he said earnestly.

'So can your father,' George added, in the same tone of voice. 'The Five are right behind you in any trouble you have with Dr Stein. I don't like the look of him one bit! And who knows – we may be able to help.'

If you didn't know George, you might have thought the girl was trying to make herself sound important, but all she was really doing was expressing the Five's love of adventure – and they did like to be useful, too. Eric knew that, and he didn't misunderstand them. He smiled at the brave little girl and pressed her hand.

36

'That's very good of you all,' he said in a low voice. 'I'm really very glad indeed you're here.'

A moment later, Stein and his bodyguards left the café and got into a big, black car which was parked not far away. They drove off, and Eric and his young friends finished their drinks and went off too, to the restaurant where they were going to have lunch. Eric said they ought to try the local Creole cookery, and ordered a special fish stew. It smelled very spicy when it came to their table, and Anne was not sure she would like it, but she had to agree with the others that it was really delicious. They ate a lovely tropical fruit salad afterwards, and then Eric took them to do some more sight-seeing in and around Fort-de-France. It was all fascinating, and Julian, listening hard, thought he was beginning to be able to understand better what the people said. 'Won't the French teacher at school be surprised if I come back next term talking Creole!' he thought.

'We'd better go back to Hibiscus Villa soon,' said Eric, late in the afternoon, 'or your parents will be wondering what I've done with you all, George. And you must be tired, too.'

The children were too excited by all they had seen and done that day to feel very tired, and they were grateful to Eric for giving up so much of his time to show them round the island. He said that before they left the capital they ought to watch the sun setting over the sea, and it really was a most impressive sight. They had never seen anything quite like it.

'You'd think the whole sea was made of golden fire!' said Anne, getting quite poetic.

Once the sun was down, it turned dark quite suddenly. Eric got behind the wheel of his car and started off along the highway. 'It won't take us long to get home,' he said, 'and then I'll –'

But they never heard what he was going to say next because at that moment a huge black car overtook him, and cut in straight in front of his car. Eric had to brake very hard. His car's tyres squealed, the car itself skidded for a moment, and then he had it under control and managed to pull up just on the edge of a big ditch by the roadside.

'What a road-hog!' said Dick indignantly. 'Fancy cutting in so dangerously right in front of us!'

'And he went straight on without stopping to see if we were all right!' said Julian. 'We might easily have gone into the ditch.'

'You know what I think?' said George, thoughtfully. '*I* think he was deliberately trying to force Eric off the road!'

The others stared at her.

'And I've got a very good idea who it was tried to make us have an accident,' she continued, 'Dr Stein! I only got a brief glimpse of the driver of that car, but I'm sure it was his face I saw behind the steering wheel.'

'And *I* saw two faces too,' said Anne, her voice trembling a little. 'Two faces looking out of the back window, and *laughing* at us. It was horrible – and I'm almost certain they belonged to Dr Stein's two bodyguards.'

'I'm afraid George may well be right,' said Eric, sighing, as he started off along the road again. 'Stein's becoming more and more dangerous. Listen, take my advice and don't get into his bad books,' he told the children. 'I'm very grateful for your offers of help, but Stein could well decide to injure you as well as us. Obviously he's furious with my father, and wants to get revenge on him. I wouldn't want anything to happen to you, just because you're staying with us! My father would never forgive himself – nor would I. I shall be on my guard after this. And I'd like you to keep out of it!'

'Keep out of it? Nothing doing!' said George firmly. 'It's not so easy to scare *us*, Eric! Not as easy as you or Dr Stein may think! If you ask me, Stein's just issued a challenge – and the Five aren't going to be such cowards as to turn it down!'

Chapter Four

HUNTING SNAKES

Next day Eric took the children on another sight-seeing tour of the island. They went bathing again, and saw some very interesting things. There was one place which was almost a desert, with bits of old, petrified trees and volcanic boulders all over it. They got there along a path which was rather difficult to walk on, and had manchineel trees growing beside it. Eric explained that the sap, the leaves and the fruits of these trees were all poisonous, and it was very dangerous to stand underneath one in the rain, because the liquid dripping off it could burn the skin.

At supper that evening, Dr Anderson said, 'I must go out snake-hunting on the slopes of Mount Pelée tomorrow – I'll take Victor with me. Three of my pit-vipers have died recently, and I need fresh venom, so I'm going to look for some new snakes myself. I've been offered some for sale, but they were not in good condition, and my suppliers were asking far too much money for them. So I'll see if I can't find some better snakes myself. There ought to be some good specimens near the crater up at the top of the mountain.'

'Oh, Paul, you will be careful, won't you?' said Mrs Anderson anxiously.

'Of course I will, my dear – and I'm no novice snake-hunter, you know! Besides, there's very little danger in broad daylight. Why, if Eric would like to come and bring his young friends, it would be an interesting outing for them,' said Dr Anderson.

'Oh, *may* we come, sir?' said Julian, delighted. 'I read about Mount Pelée before we left England, in a book that Uncle Quentin lent me. It's the volcano which exploded in 1902, isn't it?'

'That's right, Julian,' said Uncle Quentin, pleased to find that his nephew remembered. 'It was a memorable date in the history of Martinique. The town of St Pierre, which used to be the capital of the island, was covered with ash and molten lava. Thirty thousand people died there – a terrible tragedy. I'd like to see the volcano myself, Paul. I'll come with you too, if I may.'

'By all means – I'll be delighted to have your company,' said Dr Anderson. And he added, turning to the children, 'Since we're talking about snakes, you might be interested to know that they're said to have foretold the eruption of the volcano two days in advance, by leaving the

41

mountain and going off into the plains. The mass departure of snakes ought to have warned the local people to make their own escape in time, too, but unfortunately no such thing happened.'

'Did all the snakes escape the disaster, then?' Anne asked.

'Well, no,' Dr Anderson told her. 'The lava from the volcano spread so far that it buried a number of plantations, and destroyed all life on them. And in fact there have been fewer pit-vipers on the island since that eruption. However, there are still quite a lot living near the crater of the volcano, and that's where we'll go looking for them tomorrow. They're stupefied with heat at that time of day. You children can pick flowers while we're hunting snakes – you'll find that the slopes of the mountain are covered with them, growing quite close to the crater.'

George and her cousins really looked forward to the next day's expedition. They had forgotten all about the sinister Dr Stein and his bodyguards. No more had been seen or heard of him since he cut in on Eric's car so dangerously as the young people drove home from Fort-de-France. For the time being, the Five had other things to think about. Martinique really was a most interesting place!

When they all set off, the children went with Eric in his car, following a truck which belonged to the lab and carried Dr Anderson, Uncle Quentin and Victor. The truck was fitted up with special equip-

42

ment. First of all, they went across the island to Fort-de-France, to pick up two young men who were experts at catching pit-vipers.

'Now we're going to follow a road which wriggles its way from south to north through the mountainous part of the island,' said Eric. 'It takes us through the tropical rain forest.'

George and her cousins were enchanted by the sight of the forest. They had never seen such tall tress – and how very green they were, too!

'Look!' said Eric, as he drove out of the forest at last. 'There's Mount Pelée, right ahead of you.'

'Oh,' said George, sounding a bit disappointed. 'I thought it would look bigger.'

'It's just under fourteen hundred metres high,' said Eric. 'But the volcano could erupt any time, so it's not a mountain to be despised.'

The two vehicles started along a road with tall banks on either side, leading up to the lower slopes of the mountain. They stopped when this road came to an end on a kind of plateau, and everyone got out. Dr Anderson gave the children sturdy sticks. 'No need to hurry over the climb,' he said. 'You can take your time, and admire the view, and don't bother about catching up with the rest of us. Eric will look after you, and we'll see you later.'

The scientist strode off uphill, accompanied by Victor, Uncle Quentin . and the two young snake-hunters. Eric and the children started climbing the mountain too, but they didn't hurry. It wasn't a very difficult climb, though the track was a narrow one, with many gaping crevices in it, and sometimes the children had to scramble over them to get along. But there was a wonderful view, and Anne couldn't stop exclaiming with delight at the sight of the colourful flowers. Timmy chased about in all directions, and George had to call him to heel quite often.

At last the children reached the top of the mountain. The four cousins were rather disappointed once again by the sight of the crater. It was so wide and so overgrown with vegetation that there really wasn't much for them to see.

The snake-hunting party was busy doing something or other in a particularly overgrown place, some way from where Eric and the children were standing. George, who feared very little and always wanted to know what was going on, would have liked to join them and see just what they were up to, but Eric wouldn't let her.

'We'll stay here and rest,' he said firmly. 'My father has a whistle with him and, when he blows it, that means it's time for us to start the climb down again.'

And sure enough, after a while they heard the sound of a whistle. Both parties turned and made their separate ways down the mountain, to meet on the plateau where the road ended. Anne was alarmed to see a metal cage with three captured pit-vipers in it. They were writhing and hissing as

44

their ugly heads swayed to and fro.

But Victor was obviously delighted. He was smiling broadly.

'We get plenty venom now!' he said. 'And it don't cost us hardly no trouble at all!'

'Victor's right,' said Dr Anderson, sounding pleased. 'We caught our three specimens here quite quickly and quite easily.'

Mrs Anderson and Aunt Fanny had packed up an excellent picnic lunch for everybody, and when they had eaten it, they set off for the capital of the island again. Dr Anderson paid the two young snake-hunters and dropped them off in Fort-de-France, and then he and Eric and the others set off for the Caravelle peninsula and home.

They were going to take the snakes straight to the laboratory – but when they reached it, they found an unpleasant surprise waiting for them!

There was a fire engine standing outside the building, and several firemen were busy putting out the last embers of a blaze.

'My word – what on earth has been going on?' exclaimed Dr Anderson. He sounded very upset and began running towards the firemen.

The fire captain came to meet him. The pair talked in French together, but luckily Eric was able to translate it for the children. 'Nothing serious, sir, don't worry,' the fire captain was saying to Dr Anderson. 'However, the damage might have been considerable if we hadn't arrived in time. It seems

that someone deliberately set fire to the north wall of your experimental centre. The wind fanned the flames, and when the watchman spotted them he was going to call us directly, but he found the telephone wires had been cut – and the tyres of your own car, which I suppose you drove here this morning, had been slashed. The watchman had to run all the way to Tartane to let us know we were needed.'

Then he added something in very fast French. 'He's saying that the delay might have had very serious consequences for the laboratory if the place hadn't been built of specially fireproofed materials,' Eric told the children. 'If he's right, then my father was very lucky! And now he's saying something we know only too well – what with this, and the attempted burglary the other day, which they'd heard about at the fire station, he thinks my father has an enemy somewhere, and he'd better look out!'

Dr Anderson thanked the firemen, and then he hurried into the laboratory building, along with Uncle Quentin, Eric, and the Five, to see how much damage had been done. Luckily it wasn't too bad, and could be repaired quite easily.

'The insurance company will pay, of course,' said Eric, as they left the laboratory again. 'But I can guess who's behind this.'

'Dr Stein?' said Dick in an undertone.

'Who else? But he didn't actually leave a visiting

card!' said Eric.

George noticed that Timmy was sniffing at a bush a little way down the path – and then she saw a piece of fabric caught in its branches. The clever dog was trying to pick it out with his teeth. 'What are you after, Timmy, old fellow?' George asked him. 'You want that bit of stuff, do you?' And she got it out of the bush, and she was just going to let Timmy have it to play with when she noticed that it wasn't torn or even threadbare. She smoothed it out, and saw that it was a scarf made of bright red cotton.

'Hallo, what have you got there?' asked Eric, joining her. 'I say – I recognise that scarf, George. At least, if it isn't the same then it's the twin brother of the scarf one of Stein's bodyguards usually wears in the neck of his shirt. It belongs to the smaller man, the one I think of as Monkey.'

'The one who's so cunning, you mean?' asked George.

'That's right. Look at it, George – it can't have been there long. It isn't dirty or creased. If you ask me, Monkey came here on Stein's orders, and tried to set fire to the lab!'

'Then this scarf will be enough to prove he's guilty!' said George triumphantly. But Eric shook his head.

'That's what *you* think,' he said. 'A red cotton scarf isn't unusual, and you can be sure that Monkey has already gone off to get another. He's not the only man to wear such a scarf, either.'

Eric and George had been lingering behind the others, and now they hurried to catch up with them and tell them what Timmy had found. Dr Anderson shook his head sadly.

'And so it goes on!' he said, sighing. 'Stein is not the man I'd wish for as an enemy. So far, his plans have gone wrong, but luck won't always be against him, and then – well, I can't help worrying.'

In fact, it turned out that Dr Anderson was slightly wrong here – his enemy hadn't really meant to burn the laboratory down. The idea had been to show what he *could* do if he really tried, as Dr Anderson found out when the post came next morning. He opened an envelope, went rather pale as he looked at the letter inside, and then read it out to his wife and son and to his guests.

It was quite a short letter, and said, 'It would be easy enough to cause a fatal accident, instead of simply alarming the driver of a car by cutting in too soon after passing him. Similarly, it would be easy to burn a building right down instead of setting light to a few old rags which wouldn't be likely to do much damage. But don't underestimate those two incidents! They should be regarded as warnings. If we can't come to an agreement next time, something much worse is likely to happen to you. Your entire laboratory might well be burnt down. Think it over – and be careful!'

Chapter Five

A MEETING IS ARRANGED

The threatening letter had no signature.

Mrs Anderson uttered a cry of fright. 'Oh, Paul
– whatever can this mean?' she asked.

'It means that Stein has been trying to scare me,
and is capable of anything if it'll get him what he
wants,' said her husband grimly.

'You'll take that letter to the police, won't you,
sir?' said Julian. 'I mean, here's the proof you
wanted! And the police will do something about it.'

Dr Anderson sighed. 'What *could* they do? Stein
is very clever. The letter's been typed, and you can
be sure there won't be any fingerprints on it.'

'Suppose we could find the typewriter?' said
George eagerly. 'I read somewhere that you can
identify the machine used to type anything, from
damaged keys and so on.'

'You may be sure, too, that Stein knows that just
as well as you do,' Uncle Quentin pointed out.

'He'll have taken pains to use a typewriter that couldn't be traced back to him.'

'All the same,' said Dr Anderson, folding the letter up again, 'I shall certainly pass this letter on to my policeman friend, Commissaire Dupont. However, I doubt if he'll be able to do anything much. I'm afraid it's just up to me to wait until I find something convincing in the way of real proof.'

'Or until something terrible happens to all of us!' said his wife, looking very upset.

'Now, now, my dear, don't distress yourself,' said Dr Anderson. 'Stein is a dangerous man, no doubt about it, but I'm someone to be reckoned with as well, you know!'

'Listen,' cried Dick, 'if he really means to burn your laboratory down, surely you can ask the police to protect it, sir?'

'Yes, Dr Anderson,' said Anne, in her gentle voice. 'Stein will have to give up if the police are guarding the lab the whole time.'

Eric smiled kindly at the little girl. 'You haven't thought it all out, Anne – even if Father did get the police to keep watch on his laboratory, they couldn't go on guarding it for ever.'

'No,' Julian agreed. 'Sooner or later, they'd have to withdraw police protection. In other words, Stein would only have to wait, and then he could strike home once the way was clear again.'

'I have a suggestion,' said George, turning to Dr

51

Anderson. 'Seeing that you haven't got enough evidence to have Stein arrested, and we've agreed there's nothing much the police can do, why don't we keep watch on the lab ourselves?'

'Yes, and with any luck we'll catch Stein red-handed,' said Dick excitedly. '*Then* we can hand him over to the police.'

'And you can get on with your important work in peace, sir,' added Julian.

Dr Anderson looked at the children in surprise. 'Well, what kind young people you are!' he said. 'However, I really don't think there's much you children could do. This is a serious matter. Run away and play, now, and let me think!'

Eric and the children left the table, followed by Timmy. George was furious. 'Run away and play, indeed!' she said. 'Your father seems to think we're just babies, Eric! He doesn't trust us – but we want to help him, and we *could* help him, honestly we could!'

'Calm down, George!' said Eric, laughing. '*I* trust you, all of you, and I'm sure you really could be helpful – only I don't want to see you taking any risks.'

'Of course we could be helpful,' said Dick. 'We will be, too!'

'A plan of action, that's the first thing we need,' agreed his brother.

So as they lay sunbathing on the beach that day, the children and Eric tried drawing up a plan of action. Unfortunately, they couldn't think of anything that seemed a really good, feasible idea. By the time they went to bed that night they were all feeling rather discouraged.

Little did they know what the next day held in store for the whole household . . .

Lilah brought in a delicious tropical breakfast, as usual, with mangoes and pawpaws and guavas to eat, and everyone was there in the dining room except for the master of the house. 'Have you seen Dr Anderson, Lilah?' asked Mrs Anderson, rather surprised. 'He came downstairs a long time ago!'

'Oh yes, Mrs Anderson,' said Lilah. 'He take the letters, and a parcel that come in the mail, and then he go to his study, Mrs Anderson.'

'Would you go and tell him breakfast's ready, then? It's not like my husband to miss breakfast,' she told Aunt Fanny and Uncle Quentin. 'He believes it's the most important meal of the day.'

Lilah went off – and suddenly they heard her let out a piercing scream! She came hurrying back to the dining room, crying out. 'Oh, Mrs Anderson – the master, he no reply, so I open the door, and I see him, and he look dead! He look dead!'

'Dead?' gasped Mrs Anderson, going very pale as she rose to her feet.

'Oh, my dear, don't panic!' Aunt Fanny made haste to say. 'Perhaps he suddenly felt faint – let's go and see!'

They all hurried into Dr Anderson's study. He

53

was lying collapsed over his desk, head buried in his arms, and he wasn't moving.

Eric went up to his father and shook him gently, with a trembling hand. A slight groan escaped Dr Anderson's lips, but he did not open his eyes.

'At least he's alive!' said Eric, relieved. 'We must get him on his bed, quick! Lilah, will you telephone the doctor, and tell him my father seems to have had a fit of some kind?'

While the maid hurried off to phone, Uncle Quentin and Eric carried Dr Anderson to his room. Aunt Fanny and Mrs Anderson went with him. The Five were left alone in the study.

'A fit!' said Anne, alarmed. 'Oh dear – do you think it's anything serious?'

Nobody could tell her. George, however, was leaning over Dr Anderson's desk, her nose very close to a small, square, black box. She was sniffing cautiously at it. 'Here, have you seen this thing? It's got an awfully funny smell,' she told the others.

Julian and Dick sniffed it too. Dick sneezed.

'I say – it doesn't half sting the eyes and throat!' he said.

Nose to the ground, Timmy was sniffing a piece of paper lying on the floor. George picked it up, and automatically let her eyes stray to what was written on it.

'This parcel bomb might have killed you instead of simply sending you to sleep. Remember that! This is my last warning. We will meet at seven a.m.

tomorrow at Dubuch Castle, for a talk. *Bring no-one with you!*'

The last few words were underlined. 'Stein again!' George exclaimed. 'Another of his tricks. Dr Anderson hasn't had a fit – that black box was a parcel bomb and made him unconscious. Here – read this!'

Anne and her brothers read the letter too, and Dick fished the wrappings of the parcel out of the waste-paper basket.

'It's addressed in printed letters, and the paper's perfectly ordinary,' he told the others. 'According to the postmark, it was posted in Fort-de-France. Anyone at all could have actually taken it to the post office – and we can be sure Stein took care not to leave any fingerprints on the box. He really *is* a nasty piece of work, isn't he?'

'Oh, quick! Let's take this letter to Mrs Anderson!' said Anne, sensibly. 'Then at least they'll know what's the matter with poor Dr Anderson!'

It had all been very alarming, but Dr Anderson woke up two hours later, still feeling a little dizzy and with a slight headache; apart from that he said he was perfectly all right.

'When I undid the parcel, the little box opened all of a sudden, and an acrid-smelling smoke rose from it,' he told them. 'I didn't have time to read the note – I must have lost consciousness at once.'

When Dr Anderson felt better, he thought what to do next. He spent a long time deciding.

'I don't think there's any point in letting Dupont know of this latest incident in my battle of wits with Stein,' he said at last. 'He'd advise me *not* to go alone to the place where Stein wants me to meet him. I'm sure he'd post men around the Castle, hoping to catch the rascal – but Stein is far too clever not to have taken precautions to prevent that sort of thing. He insists on seeing me alone. I fear that if I warn the police, and he discovers they're on the spot, as I'm sure he would, we should be facing goodness knows what kind of reprisals as revenge for my failing to do as he stipulated. I really think the best thing will be for me to go and meet the man, and have the private conversation he wants.'

'But what good could come of it, Paul?' asked Mrs Anderson anxiously. 'You know that you could never consent to letting him have your formulae – and there's no possible way in which the two of you can agree!'

'Well, I still might be able to make him see reason,' said Dr Anderson.

'I doubt it, you know,' Eric told his father. 'Still, it's better to try than to rule it out completely. Anyway, I'm coming with you!'

'You are doing no such thing, Eric! I'm going on my own!'

And Dr Anderson stuck to his guns. George had what she thought was a clever idea, and suggested that he could take a pocket recorder and put the conversation on tape. Dr Anderson smiled.

'I haven't got a recorder small enough to go undetected, my dear, and though I know such things are available I couldn't get hold of one today, in a great hurry. Moreover, that kind of recording has no legal value,' he told her. 'No, I would rather meet Stein just as he says and try to come to a sensible agreement with him.'

A little later, Eric and the Five were holding a council of war in the garden of Hibiscus Villa.

'My father's mistaken if he thinks he can come to any reasonable agreement with Stein, I'm afraid,' said Eric. 'I feel very uneasy about this meeting.'

Julian had been thinking.

'Listen, I've got an idea,' he said. 'We can feel pretty certain that Stein will make sure the police aren't setting any kind of trap for him, and your father really has come to the meeting place alone. I expect he'll get those bodyguards of his to watch the surroundings of the Castle, and let him know if anyone suspicious turns up.'

'Yes!' said George, excitedly. She saw what her cousin was driving at! 'But who would be suspicious of children just wanting to play on the beach in the bay below the Castle?'

'What do you mean?' asked Eric, puzzled, looking from George to Julian and back again.

'We mean we'll get up very early tomorrow and go for a morning walk near Dubuch Castle. We'll go down to the beach – and then climb up again, very quietly, and hide as close to the meeting place itself as we possibly can,' George explained. A sudden thought occurred to her. 'I say – will they be speaking English?'

'Yes,' said Eric. 'Whatever Stein's real nationality, English seems to be his usual language. I've heard him speak it with my father. But I don't see –'

'That's just it!' Julian told him. 'Even if we don't get close enough to hear anything, we'll be able to *see* them. And that might be no bad thing for your father, Eric, old fellow!'

'But Stein and Monkey and the other man – Hercules, I call him, because he's so big – well, they'd recognise me!' said Eric.

'Of course they would. You won't be with us,' Dick told him firmly.

'It really would be too dangerous for you, Eric,' said Anne in her soft little voice.

'But *we* don't risk anything to speak of,' George finished. 'I shouldn't think those men would recognise us. They only saw us once, at a distance, in Fort-de-France, and it was you they were interested in at the time, Eric. Anyway, we'll do our best not to let them see us.'

Eric tried hard to persuade the Five to abandon their plan, but all the children thought it was a very good one, and they weren't giving way. The young man was very anxious – he felt reponsible for his friends. However, he did trust the Five, knowing how clever they could be. It was just possible that their help really might be of use to his father, in Dr Anderson's battle of wits with the rascally Dr Stein.

In the end, he realised that in any case there was nothing he could do to stop them going to the Castle.

But what really *would* happen at that meeting next morning?

Chapter Six

AND THE FIVE ATTEND IT!

Next morning George, her cousins and Timmy left
Hibiscus Villa very early and very quietly. Obviously Eric couldn't drive them to the Castle
above the bay – the sound of a car's engine would
have attracted the attention of the grown-ups at
the villa, not to mention Dr Stein and his bodyguards themselves, if they were already in position.
So he had managed to find his young friends three
bicycles – his own, and two belonging to his
parents. George and Dick had a bicycle each, and
Julian rode the third, with Anne balancing on the
cross-bar.

'And you'll just have to run along after us,
Timmy, old chap,' said George. 'I expect you'd
quite like a nice run in the cool morning air!'

It was still dark when the children set off, but the
sun rose at about six o'clock, as was usual on
Martinique, and soon drove the shadows away.

61

The road was a bit rough and bumpy, but they pedalled hard, and after a while the ruins of the Castle loomed up to the right of them. Suddenly George, who was in the lead, saw what looked like the figure of a huge statue at the end of the road ahead. She recognised Stein's bodyguard, the man Eric called Hercules. He wasn't looking their way just then – he was bending over to get something out of the back of that big black car.

'Quick!' George told the others. 'This way!'

She had already jumped off her bicycle and was pushing it through the bushes on her right.

'Let's leave the bikes here,' she whispered as her cousins followed suit. 'Now we'll climb down to the bay, and then we can come back up to the Castle!'

It wasn't the easiest of climbs, either way, but the children were glad not to have been spotted – or at least to have aroused no suspicion if they *had* been seen on their way down to the beach – and they managed it all nimbly and fast. At a quarter to seven, they were making their way towards the Castle from the south. As they tiptoed forward in single file, bending over and making as little noise as possible, Julian, who was in front, suddenly stopped.

The others followed his example. They all craned their necks to see what he had seen – and there were Stein and Monkey a little way ahead of them. They seemed to be coming out of the old dungeons where the slaves had once been housed.

The children guessed they had been making sure there were no policemen hiding there. The wind was blowing the right way for them to hear Stein's voice.

'Nobody in there – good. Looks as if we're in the clear. Simon, I want you to go and join Felix, and the pair of you can stay on guard.'

It was a relief to hear him speaking English to his bodyguard – that made it almost certain that they'd be able to understand anything he said to Dr Anderson, so long as they could get within earshot.

Monkey, otherwise known as Simon, went off at once. The four cousins hid behind the stout trunks of some trees and watched Stein climbing a slope. He stopped on a wide terrace in front of the ruined Castle, and began pacing up and down.

Dick glanced at his watch. 'Ten to seven,' he whispered. 'Dr Anderson shouldn't be long now.'

George was talking to Timmy in an undertone, telling him to keep still. His coat was bristling – he seemed to want to hurl himself at the men he had seen. Instinct told him they were his enemies.

'Ssh, old fellow!' George whispered. 'We don't want anyone to spot us! Good dog, Timmy – keep quiet. Good dog!'

'Are we going to stay here?' Anne asked in a low voice.

'Not likely!' said Dick, in the same tone. He pointed to some stone pillars which must once have been part of the big building, and were dotted about the grassy ground here and there. 'If we dodge from pillar to pillar, they'll give us cover on our way to the dungeons Stein has just been exploring.'

'Oh, I see! As he's already inspected them, he'll never think there could be anyone there!' said Anne.

'That's the idea,' Julian agreed. 'Come on, everyone – here we go!'

Taking very great care, and moving from one pillar to the next as Dick had suggested, the children made their way to the dungeons. Timmy kept very close to George. Once they got there they could breathe again.

'I say – we couldn't have found a better hiding place,' said Julian, pleased. 'We can see everything that goes on up on that terrace, from here. With a bit of luck we'll even be able to overhear the conversation.'

'Stein's still on his own.' George remarked.

'Ssh!' Julian whispered. 'I can hear footsteps. Yes, here comes Dr Anderson!'

Eric's father had just appeared on the terrace, where his adversary was waiting for him.

'Good, good!' cried Dr Stein, pretending to be very jovial. 'Glad to see you – and glad to see you've had the sense to come on your own, my dear fellow!'

The sarcasm in Stein's voice annoyed Dr Ander-

son. 'I realise I'm probably just wasting my time, trying to make you see reason,' he said. 'But I thought it was worth the effort one last time!'

The children, in their hiding place, were delighted to find that the wind was blowing their way. They couldn't catch all the words, but they got the general drift of the conversation. What a good idea of theirs to have come!

Dr Anderson, who was usually such a kind, patient man, seemed to be seething with barely controlled rage. They could guess that the mere sight of the other man infuriated him. 'I should like to know,' he was saying, 'just why you are so anxious to meet me. You know very well that I shall never do as you ask! I have not yet finished working on my formulae, and even if I had I wouldn't dream of selling them to you. As for going into partnership with you, I know you far too well ever to agree. I have the lowest possible opinion of your character and your ability!'

'If you believe you'll get anywhere by insulting me, you can think again!' said Dr Stein, laughing. 'I don't care a bit for your opinion of me! I'm a practical man, and I know what I want. Just now I have a once-in-a-lifetime chance to do a deal with a big foreign laboratory. Who cares if the work on your medicinal drugs isn't quite finished yet? All I'm asking is, how much do you want for your formulae?'

'Are you deaf?' asked Dr Anderson angrily. 'For

the last time, I tell you I am not doing business with you.'

'My offer was a genuine one, Anderson,' said the other man. 'But remember – I take what I cannot buy!'

'Is that a threat?'

'Well, you know what I can do . . . I've given you a few foretastes of it, haven't I? However, if they don't convince you, I shall have to go further.'

'So you're declaring war, are you?'

'If you like!' Dr Stein didn't sound jovial any longer. He spoke harshly, and the children could tell he was a cold, cruel man. All he lived for was money – and he wouldn't stop at anything to get it.

They shivered as they lurked in their hiding place. 'I'm scared!' whispered Anne. 'I'm afraid he's going to attack Dr Anderson!'

'No, he won't, Anne,' Julian whispered back. 'That wouldn't get him anywhere.'

'Ssh!' hissed George.

Up on the terrace Dr Stein was saying, through his teeth, 'I shall take what you refuse to give me – and neither you nor anybody else will be able to prevent me. What's more, there were no witnesses to this conversation, so any accusations you may make will do you no good!'

'We'll see about that,' whispered Dick. 'There *were* witnesses! Us! We've got you now, Dr Stein! We can give evidence against you.'

Julian sighed. 'You're forgetting we're only

67

children, Dick,' he reminded his brother. 'Our evidence wouldn't carry much weight in a court of law, I'm afraid.'

'Then that dreadful man is going to get the better of Eric's father?' whispered Anne, almost in tears.

'Looks like it,' said Dick gloomily. 'What do you think, George?' he whispered, turning to his cousin.

But George wasn't there any more, and nor was Timmy.

'Hallo!' said Dick. 'Where can they have gone?'

'Ssh – not so loud! They'll hear us,' Julian whispered.

The two men were turning away from each other over on the terrace. Dr Anderson strode angrily off towards the road. A moment later, they heard a car engine starting, and realised he was leaving. They guessed he would be going straight to his laboratory at the end of the peninsula.

Julian, Dick and Anne, still hiding in the shelter of one of the slave dungeons, dared not move yet. And they were all wondering rather anxiously where George and Timmy could be. They hadn't actually seen the two of them leave. What on earth had come over George? It seemed a very rash thing to do – what was her idea?

'Let's get out of here,' said Dick, moving to go.

But Julian held him back. 'Hang on a minute longer. We'll let Stein get a good start, and then follow him. We might learn something else about him. Anyway, we can't go back down towards the bay, not with that villain and his two bodyguards about to leave themselves.'

So they waited until Stein had gone, and then hurried up the grassy slope to the terrace. Once they reached it, they turned left and made for the road, going carefully and hiding behind some thorny bushes. Soon they were within sight of the big, black car. Sure enough, the two bodyguards were there, waiting for their boss. The children saw Stein cross the road to join them.

He opened his mouth to say something – he was talking energetically and gesticulating, as if to emphasise his words. Monkey and Hercules, otherwise Simon and Felix, seemed to be agreeing with him.

Dick bit back an exclamation of disappointment. The wind had changed, and there was too much distance between the children and the three men for the former to be able to hear what the latter were saying. 'Bother!' thought the boy. 'Our luck's changed – just like the wind itself.'

Stein got into the car, with Simon beside him. Felix got behind the wheel, and they started off. In a moment or so, the sinister trio had disappeared down the road.

As soon as they knew they were on their own, Julian, Dick and Anne emerged on to the road themselves. The conversation between Dr Anderson and Stein had really shaken them. They realised that there was bitter enmity between the two scientists – if Dr Stein was really worthy of that name – and they saw a merciless struggle looming ahead. What was worse, they didn't see just *how* they could help kind Dr Anderson.

They had another and more immediate problem, too. 'Where on earth *is* George?' asked Dick once more.

'Here I am!' said a voice. And George's mischievous face appeared between a couple of bushes at the roadside, just where Dr Stein's car had been standing.

'My goodness!' said Anne. 'Is that where you and Timmy have been hiding? But how –'

'How did I get here?' said George, clambering out of the bushes. 'Easy! When I realised neither Dr Anderson nor Dr Stein was at all likely to give way, I thought it was pretty pointless to go on listening to their argument. And if I moved somewhere else I had more chance of learning something useful.'

'So that's when you left us, was it?' asked Julian.

'Yes – I went a little way way round, and got to the side of the road opposite the car very quietly, without being noticed.'

'Then what?' asked Julian, rather cross with himself for letting George slip away on her own and walk into possible danger.

'Well, then I waited for Simon and that hefty

70

great brute Felix to be looking the other way, and *crossed* the road! No need to look at me like that, Ju – they didn't spot me. They just went on talking – they were hardly keeping watch at all. It was easy.'

'What happened next?' asked Anne. She admired George's courage enormously, though she felt her cousin was sometimes dreadfully rash.

'Next I slithered down into the ditch, and then I climbed up again into the bushes the other side of it. I was so close to the car that I could hear every word Stein's bodyguards were saying.'

'And what *were* they saying?' asked Julian, with bated breath.

George laughed. 'I said I could hear every word – I didn't say I could understand it! They speak English to Stein all right, but they speak French to each other, and I think it was that funny sort of Creole French too. At least, I couldn't make any of it out.'

'That's a pity,' said Julian, but he was more worried about George. 'George, suppose they'd found you!'

George grinned happily. 'They didn't! And I had Timmy to protect me, didn't I?'

'Woof!' said Timmy, and even Julian couldn't help laughing.

'Oh well – all's well that ends well, even if you took the most enormous risks, and never learned anything in the end!' he said.

George grinned again. 'Who says I didn't learn

anything?' she asked. 'I jolly well did! I found out when Stein means to launch his attack!'

Chapter Seven

ON GUARD

George's cousins looked at her in astonishment.

'But you said just now you couldn't understand what the bodyguards were saying,' Dick pointed out.

'Not when they were talking to each other, no. But they spoke English to Dr Stein. And when he came back to them he let slip his plan,' said George happily. 'I can tell you just what he said, word for word. "That fool Anderson – he's as obstinate as a mule. But he'll soon find out what I can do! In fact we'll show him this very night. Once we've finished with that lab of his, he'll have to apply for a grant to build another and start from scratch!" And then he laughed, in a nasty sort of way.'

Anne had turned pale. 'Oh, George – it sounds as if they're going to do something dreadful to damage the laboratory!'

'It does,' said her cousin grimly. 'And tonight, too!'

'Well, come on – we must go and warn Dr Anderson!' said Julian.

And all the others agreed that there was no time to be wasted. When they reached the laboratory, the scientist was hard at work. He was in rather a bad temper too. He sighed when old Victor knocked on the door of his office and told him the children were there. 'Really, I could do without those young people just now!' he said rather crossly. 'It's easy to see *they* have nothing to do but amuse themselves. Oh, tell them I haven't got time to see them at the moment, Victor. I can't understand Eric, letting them come and disturb me like this.'

'Mr Eric, he not with them, doctor,' said Victor. 'And that little lady who look like a boy, she say it very, very urgent!'

George had rather expected that Dr Anderson wouldn't feel much like seeing them; she was sure he was in a bad mood after his conversation with Stein. So she had followed close behind Victor, and her cousins followed *her*. She reached the open door of the office just as Dr Anderson was saying, 'Well, I've no time to spare now. Ask them to go away, Victor, and then perhaps I can get some work done in peace.'

George walked boldly into the office. 'Dr Anderson,' she said, 'I'm awfully sorry to disturb you –

but there really *isn't* any time to spare. That's why we came!'

Dr Anderson looked absolutely baffled.

'You see,' George said earnestly, 'Stein is planning to destroy your laboratory, and he means to do it this evening.'

It was a real bombshell! Dr Anderson stared at her, stunned, and Victor's mouth dropped open with astonishment.

'What on earth do you mean, George?' Dr Anderson asked brusquely. 'Explain yourself, please!'

So she did, and her cousins backed her up. Timmy stood there watching Dr Anderson with his head on one side, wagging his tail gently, just as if he were saying, 'We're good sleuths, we are!'

When the children had finished telling their story, Dr Anderson rose from his chair and solemnly shook hands with each of them.

'You are very good children,' he said. He was obviously deeply touched. 'I ought to scold you for acting so rashly, but you have done me such a great service that I can only thank you with all my heart!'

Then he started thinking what to do. His assistants, and all the rest of the laboratory staff, were told what had happened, and it was decided that teams of them would take turns to stay on guard in the laboratory that night. Dr Anderson himself would stay there all night, and would not go home to bed at all.

The children and Dr Anderson went back to Hibiscus Villa for lunch, and told Eric, Mrs Anderson, Aunt Fanny and Uncle Quentin what had happened. 'I'll go up to the laboratory and spend the night with you, of course,' Uncle Quentin told his friend.

'Thanks, Quentin,' said Dr Anderson. 'I'll be glad of your company.'

Eric and the children would have liked to be there too, but Uncle Quentin said a firm no, so far as George and her cousins were concerned, and Eric tactfully dropped his own idea of going so that the children wouldn't feel too bad about it.

'You've done enough for one day!' Uncle Quentin told them. 'And done it very well, too. Now you can leave the matter in our hands. You were up very early this morning – you'll be needing a good night's sleep.'

It was going to be hard to sleep at all, the children thought, knowing that *anything* might be happening at the laboratory! They watched gloomily as Uncle Quentin and Dr Anderson drove off that evening. When they went to bed, they tossed and turned, and found it almost impossible to doze off. They kept wondering just what was going on at Devil's Point at that moment. Had Stein launched his attack on the building? Timmy was the only one who slept well that night, snoring happily till dawn.

76

At breakfast next morning, they learned from the two men that nothing unusual had happened at the laboratory after all. They were pleased but a little disappointed.

'It's funny,' said George, pouring herself a glass of fruit juice. 'Do you think Stein decided to put it off, or what?'

'Well, we'll keep watch again tonight,' said Dr Anderson, buttering a piece of toast. 'George, are you quite sure of what Stein said to his body-guards?'

'Positive!' said George decidedly.

'I'll say this for my daughter, she has excellent hearing!' said Uncle Quentin. 'We can rely on the accuracy of what she told us.'

'You know,' said Julian, 'it seems to me that Stein may have been speaking in the heat of the moment when he told the men he was going to attack the laboratory last night. He was very angry, wasn't he?'

Everyone, including Dr Anderson, nodded.

'Well, he must have thought better of it, and decided to take his time over planning what to do.'

'Oh, dear!' sighed Mrs Anderson. 'How I wish that dreadful man was safely behind bars! All this is such a strain on my nerves!'

'Don't worry, Mother,' said Eric. 'I doubt if he'll wait much longer before he acts – and then we'll catch him!'

'But Paul, wouldn't it be best to tell the police?'

Aunt Fanny asked.

'Well, it's rather tricky,' said the scientist. 'If the police set a trap at Devil's Point, you can be sure Stein will get to hear of it, and he'll lie low. So the simplest thing is to let him believe we know nothing of his intentions – and to be on our guard!'

'Yes, I see,' said Aunt Fanny, nodding.

Nothing happened the next night either – or for three nights after that. Stein was obviously waiting before his next move after all. 'I think he must have got wind of the way we're guarding the laboratory,' said Dr Anderson. 'With any luck, he's decided to give up the attempt to damage it.'

George and her cousins didn't agree – and they were dismayed when Dr Anderson said he thought he could stop sleeping at the lab, and there was no need for the staff to keep such a careful watch any more. After all, Victor was always there to act as night watchman.

'I can see that my father doesn't like to ask the staff to keep on mounting guard, when nothing at all seems to happen!' said Eric. 'I suspect he's also beginning to think George may have been mistaken in what she heard, after all.'

'Or that I'm just making it up so as to seem important, I suppose!' said George, crossly.

'No, no, George,' Eric assured her. 'He knows you never tell lies.'

'Your father knows what Dr Stein's like,' said

Dick. 'That ought to be enough to persuade him not to be careless.'

'Well, he trusts Victor – and the lab has a good alarm system.'

'That's all very well,' said Julian, sounding anxious, 'but Victor's old, and it's not all that hard to put an alarm system out of action.'

That evening, as if by common consent, the Five met in the garden of Hibiscus Villa. They all had the same worry on their minds. 'You know, I think Dr Anderson's being rash,' said Dick, saying what everyone was thinking. 'And there's no time to lose if we're going to protect him.'

'Exactly my own opinion,' said George.

'Then let's draw up a plan,' suggested Julian.

Timmy obviously thought this was a good idea, for he barked enthusiastically.

'Yes, but what sort of a plan?' Anne asked.

Well, that was quite a question! The children spent a long time discussing it, and in the end they came to a conclusion which they didn't really like very much, since it meant acting in what they were afraid would be thought of as a deceitful way by the grown-ups, and they hated even to *seem* to be deceitful.

'Still, there's nothing for it,' said Dick. 'If we asked permission they'd say no!'

So later that evening, when everyone thought the children had gone to bed, they slipped silently out of the villa, found the bicycles in the Ander-

sons' garage, and started out along the road to the end of the peninsula.

They had been bicycling several times over the last few days, and a fourth cycle had been borrowed from friends of the Andersons for Anne, but she was a little scared to be pedalling along in the middle of the night – and Timmy wasn't entirely happy either. He knew there was something different about this West Indian road. It didn't smell like the roads at home, and the creatures whose scent he picked up weren't the English rabbits he was so fond of chasing.

However, the five kilometres to the laboratory weren't really very far to go. When they got there, Julian rang the bell beside the main door of the building. Someone looked out through a little window set in the door at about the level of a man's eyes.

'Who there so late as this?' a voice asked.

'Victor – it's us!' said George. 'Open the door, quick! We've come to help you keep watch tonight.'

'You come right along in!' said Victor, pleased, opening the door wide. 'Why, you real good children, come to keep me company like this!' The good-hearted old man was touched by their kind thought, and never stopped to think if they had asked permission to be out. They were there; that was enough for him, and he welcomed them warmly.

While Julian started going round to check all the alarms, George, Dick and Anne inspected the separate laboratories and the other rooms in the building, making sure the windows were well closed. Victor went with them, smiling.

'I already check, myself!' he assured them. 'But you go ahead if you like!'

'It can't hurt, anyway,' said Dick.

'We got the alarms, boy,' Victor reminded him.

Well, the fact was that the children didn't have a great deal of confidence in the alarm system which Victor trusted so much. They thought it would be safer to go round the building from time to time, keeping watch in relays. Anne and Julian would take the 'first watch', then it would be Dick, George and Timmy, and finally Victor. If the old man's turn was last, he could get a good night's rest.

'And when Victor takes over we'll go back to Hibiscus Villa as quietly as we came,' said Julian. 'With luck nobody will suspect we ever went out.'

'And we're coming back again tomorrow night, aren't we, Julian?' said Anne.

'Yes – we'll have a lie-in late in the morning to make up for it!' Dick reminded the others.

'I bet everyone tells us how lazy we are!' said George, grinning.

Julian and his little sister took the first watch, as agreed. They walked quietly round the building, looking into each room once every half an hour.

When they were sure that everything was all right, they went back to the entrance hall, their point of departure, and played cards until they thought it was time to set off again. They didn't really concentrate on their card game – their ears were pricked for any unusual sounds.

But nothing happened. After three hours, Julian and Anne went to wake George and Dick, who were sleeping on the two beds in the little laboratory sick-room.

George and Dick were on their feet at once and ready for action. So was good old Timmy!

'Nothing to report,' said Julian. 'Perhaps Stein really has given up his plan after all.'

'I somehow don't think so,' said George, making for the doorway.

As they were passing the little glassed-in cubicle where Victor was sleeping, the cousins couldn't help smiling. The old man was snoring like a grampus!

'Well, if Stein happens to be around, *that* ought to encourage him to show his hand!' said George. 'Anyone could hear that the night watchman's asleep a mile off!'

She and Dick started conscientiously going their first round. Once they had completed it, they came back to the hall, as Julian and Anne had done – but no sooner had they got there than Timmy ran to the door, nose to the ground, and began growling quietly.

Chapter Eight

ATTACK AND COUNTER-ATTACK

George stole towards him on tiptoe. 'Ssh, Timmy! Quiet – good dog! Did you hear something?' she whispered.

'Grr!' said Timmy again, in a low tone.

'I expect he's picked up the scent of a mongoose,' said Dick. 'There are lots around here, and Timmy thinks they're rats.'

'I'm not so sure,' said George. 'Listen . . .'

Dick listened. He heard a very slight sound, like something brushing past the outside of the double doors. And at the same moment, a cautious footstep made the gravel on the path outside crunch slightly. The boy glanced out through the little window set into the door.

'There's somebody out there,' he whispered.

'Stay here, Timmy. Stay!' George told her dog. 'And bark if anyone tries coming in, understand?'

'Woof!' said the intelligent Timmy, pricking up his ears.

'Come on, Dick,' said George. 'Let's go upstairs. We'll be able to see what's going on better from the first floor.'

It didn't take them a moment to run up the stairs. Quietly and cautiously, they opened a window and leaned out. Just below them, three shadowy figures were up to something mysterious and obviously sinister outside the entrance to the building.

'Quick!' breathed George. 'Let's go and wake the others.'

In a moment the decks were cleared for action! The children found Victor in a state of great dismay – he had just discovered that the telephone wires had been cut, and so he couldn't warn Dr Anderson that something was going on. Victor was a brave old man – but it would take more than courage to defend the whole laboratory building against this crafty attack.

Suddenly, Timmy let out a loud, 'Woof! Woof! Woof!' His barking was amplified by the dimensions of the entrance hall and went echoing out into the night. The sinister, quiet sounds outside had stopped. But it was likely to take more than the chance of meeting a fierce dog inside to stop the enemy.

George, Julian, Dick and Anne stood there looking at each other for a moment or so, feeling almost as much at a loss as Victor did. They had spotted the enemy all right, at the very moment when the attack was being launched – but just spotting him wasn't really enough. A little late in the day, the children realised, with horror, that they hadn't thought what to do to counter Stein's attack when it came. Without consciously realising it, they had probably been banking on being able to summon help by telephone.

'What we do now?' asked Victor suddenly. Timmy's barking was getting on his nerves. 'Those rascals maybe set fire to this whole building.'

That was just what the children were thinking too, and they had no intention of being roasted alive inside the building with all its ultra-modern equipment.

'I know what!' said George suddenly. 'We'll start by throwing things down on the enemy, the same way as people did in the Middle Ages when their castles were being besieged. Come on!'

She dashed back to the first floor with her cousins after her. As she passed, she snatched up anything heavy enough to serve as a missile, and Anne followed her example.

Julian and Dick each took one of the fire extinguishers that stood at either end of the corridor.

'Here goes!' shouted George at the top of her voice.

Down below in the hall, Timmy was still barking furiously, and Victor had struck up what sounded like a kind of war song.

All together, the four cousins leaned out of the first-floor windows and launched their counter-offensive.

Stein, Felix and Simon, who had begun sprinkling petrol around the bottom of the double doors, suddenly felt as if the sky were falling on their heads! George and Anne were bombarding them with all sorts of unexpected missiles, while Julian and Dick, standing at another window, were spraying them with a fire extinguisher and a hose hastily attached to a tap in a wash basin. All the children aimed so well you might have thought they were trained firemen and gunners.

The three men outside had just lit a fire, but the four cousins put that out at once – and the men themselves, drenched with water, fending off missiles and blinded with extinguisher foam, had to beat a retreat.

'We did it!' cried Dick. 'We've driven them off!'

'But they'll be back,' said Julian, less cheerfully. 'Or else they'll attack from more than one side of the building, and we can't be everywhere at once. We haven't got any means of defence against them either. We're just children, and one old man, without any kind of weapons!'

'I've got an idea,' said George.

Serious as the situation was, her cousins couldn't help smiling. George so often 'got an idea' at the crucial moment. Her clever little brain

always seemed to work well under pressure, and she had often come up with the answer to some very tricky questions!

'You've got an idea?' said Dick. 'Never!'

'We'll act the way people do in Westerns,' said George, taking no notice of him. 'You know what I mean – when the brave pioneer and his family are surrounded by a tribe of Indians on the warpath.'

'What do they do about it?' asked Julian, rather sarcastically.

'Well, you know how when they want to make the enemy think there are more of them than there really are, they fire guns out of all the windows – the pioneer at one window, and his wife and children all at different ones?'

'Yes,' said Dick. 'What about it?'

'Well, if Stein and company are going to attack the lab at several points all at once, as Julian suggested, we'll be ready to show them we're on guard everywhere too,' said George.

'You've forgotten that we haven't any guns,' said Dick.

'And no weapons of any other kind either,' Anne pointed out.

'Oh, never mind that!' said George. 'The main thing is to make them *think* we're able to defend ourselves. They won't see our weapons, but they'll *hear* them all right!'

'George has finally gone off her head,' said Dick, shaking his.

'Not yet!' said George, smiling. 'Victor can show us where the spare electric light bulbs are kept. There's bound to be a big stock of them in a place like this. We'll arm ourselves with light bulbs, stand at the windows on all four sides of the building and throw them out. They ought to make a good noise smashing!'

'George, that's a brilliant idea!' cried Julian. 'Yes, that may do it, but we must be very careful not actually to hit anyone.'

'But will that really be enough to frighten Dr Stein off?' asked Anne.

'We can try it, anyway,' said her big brother. 'And we'll call out orders to imaginary reinforcements. Bluff sometimes pays off! It's possible that Dr Stein, who thinks we're alone, will come to suspect that Dr Anderson's turned the tables on him and taken secret precautions. If so, he may lift his siege, but we can still prove he tried to burn the laboratory down. Victor will confirm what we have to say.'

Soon they were armed with light bulbs and not a moment too soon! Dr Stein and his men were just about to launch a second and even more ferocious attack, just as Julian had expected. However, the besieged defenders were ready for them. Suddenly, something seemed to explode in the ears of Stein, Simon and Felix, and dust flew up from the ground close to them!

The three men wondered what on earth was

going on – how were they to know the noise was made by nothing worse than the shattering of electric light bulbs?

There was a second burst of 'firing', and they retreated again, drawing back into the cover of the trees to consult each other. Dick left the window where he was stationed for a moment, to go and find his cousin.

'George, I don't think Stein and his friends are going to fall for this bluff of ours much longer,' he said, worried. 'Stein's no fool, you know.'

'No, I know,' George agreed. 'We'll have to think of something else, and pretty fast. But what? After all, it's not very likely that Stein really means to burn us alive inside the laboratory! He just wants to force us out so that he can set fire to it at his leisure. We're not giving in, though! Still, you're right – we must think of something else. The trouble is, my mind's a blank!'

For once, George's imagination had let her down. Suddenly the children heard Victor's voice raised on the ground floor. He was shouting defiantly at the men outside.

'You just get out of here fast!' the old man was calling through the little window set into the door, 'or old Victor here set the doctor's snakes on you!'

'My word – I believe he would, too!' said Dick, in alarm.

'No, he wouldn't,' said George. 'That would make things even worse than they are now. Get back to your window, Dick. I think I can see someone moving about in the dark down below.'

It was Felix, moving along the right wing of the building with a bundle of dried grass for kindling. But George had spotted him. Taking aim, she threw a light bulb. Smash! It broke to bits nearby.

But Felix only laughed, and went on with what he was doing.

'Oh, bother!' said George. 'He's realised what we're up to!'

In her fury, she picked up a chair and threw it out of the window at the man. Felix let out a yell, and retreated. But George had seen him flick his cigarette lighter and set fire to the dry grass first.

And at that very moment Victor, obviously thinking *he* had had a good idea, flung the double doors open and told the excited Timmy, 'Go on – you good dog, go on! Bite them, good dog, bite them!'

Timmy could have asked for nothing better! He began by making for Simon, who was standing just outside. Simon the Monkey wasn't a bit brave – he turned and ran for his life.

Timmy dashed round the corner of the laboratory building and leaped at Felix. George, leaning out of the window, was just emptying a fire extinguisher over the flames the big man had lit. She was so horrified to see Timmy appear that she let go of the extinguisher, which fell right on top of Felix. Stunned, he fell to the ground.

And now Timmy, delighted to have overcome two of his enemies, was making for Dr Stein! Stein was busy sprinkling petrol along the back of the building, and George lost sight of the dog. Horrified to think of the risk her beloved Timmy might be running, she leaned a little farther out of the window, calling to him. 'Timmy! Come back, Timmy! Tim, come back, old boy!'

Too late! At that very moment, Timmy was rushing at Stein, who had seen him coming. With a swift gesture, he threw his jacket over the dog's head, blinding him. Taken by surprise, Timmy stopped dead, and then he heard George calling him. He tried to turn round, but he couldn't shake off the jacket, which had caught in the buckle of his collar.

Frantic, Timmy made his way back into the laboratory. Victor was holding the door open. But instead of running up to join George on the first floor, the dog raced blindly through all the rooms on the ground floor, rubbing against everything he met in an attempt to get rid of the jacket. It was still half blinding him, and he was frightened of it.

He reached the room where the snakes were kept, and flung himself so hard against the bench on which a glass case was standing that he overturned the whole thing; the bolt holding the lid in place slipped back, and the captive pit-viper, suddenly freed, obviously thought it would take advantage of the confusion to slide over the tiled floor and look for a way of escape.

Victor, following Timmy, had seen the whole thing. Keeping his presence of mind, he managed to snatch the jacket off Timmy's head and throw it over the snake.

'There — now I put you back!' he told the pit-viper. The children arrived at that moment, brought downstairs by Timmy's wild barking. They were full of alarm, and admiration for Victor's brave act.

'Careful, Victor!' said Julian. 'Do watch out!'

'You get back!' Victor told him. 'I can handle him!'

Moving fast, he grabbed the snake through the fabric of the jacket, and was about to put it back in its case. But the snake wasn't playing. With a furious hiss, it poked its head out from under the jacket, and turned to strike at the hand holding it. It sank its venomous fangs into Victor's thumb.

George and her cousins gasped with terror. But Victor calmly got the snake back into its case, and bolted the lid into position over it.

'Victor!' cried Anne. 'It bit you!'

'Yes, miss,' said Victor. 'The doctor have to give me an injection now. We got plenty anti-venom serum, but I don't know how Dr Anderson use it!'

The children looked at each other. *They* didn't know how to give an injection of serum either . . . and Dr Anderson was five kilometres away, in Hibiscus Villa.

Chapter Nine

GEORGE GETS SOME MORE IDEAS

'Eric told us the antidote has to be injected without delay,' said Julian, going rather pale.

'It's a matter of life or death!' Dick agreed, in a low voice. He was feeling stunned too.

'I've got an i –' George began. But then she suddenly stopped short, and cried, 'Well, it's no good standing here, we must *do* something! Victor, you go and lie down on your bed and keep perfectly still. Julian, Dick, Anne – go back up to the first floor and make as much noise as you can. Yell and scream! Do all you possibly can to attract the enemy's attention. And meanwhile I'll –'

'Meanwhile you'll do what?' asked Dick.

But by that time George was out of the room. The girl would do anything to save kind old Victor. 'Follow me, Timmy!' she told her dog. 'You can protect me if necessary.'

When she reached the main doors she stopped to

listen. A tremendous row suddenly broke out overhead, as the others yelled and shouted. 'Good!' murmured George to herself, smiling. 'They're doing well up there! Now I must seize my chance while Stein and his men are wondering what's going on in the laboratory.'

Sure enough, surprised by the row Julian, Dick and Anne were kicking up, Stein and his henchmen were staring at the laboratory building's windows, where they could see the shadowy figures of the three children moving about. George made her way out of the building without being seen. With Timmy close behind her, she ran to Stein's big car.

'Oh, good!' she said to herself. 'They've left the keys in the car!'

Of course, George was much too young to drive a car, but she had always been interested in watching other people drive, and knew what you had to do with the controls. She hoped she'd be able to start the car up and hold on to the steering wheel for a few minutes – just long enough to get away! 'The main thing is to start off as fast as I safely can,' she thought. 'Then they won't be able to catch me. Thank goodness the road's pretty straight from here to Hibiscus Villa!'

George got into the driver's seat, and Timmy got in beside her. She turned the ignition key and the engine started up. George could hear shouts of rage behind her – the noise had told Stein and his men what was going on. With a jerk, the car moved forward.

George never knew how she managed to reach Hibiscus Villa safely. Driving a car was more difficult than it looked when her father did it! Very luckily, the road was quite deserted at this time of night. Concentrating hard, and thinking of Victor, who so urgently needed help, she at last reached the Andersons' house, after a very bumpy drive.

When she got there, she wasn't quite sure how to stop, and even though she was going as slowly as she possibly could the car brushed against the gatepost before coming to a halt. It made a most alarming sound, and everyone in the house got up to see what the matter was, but George hardly gave them time to say a thing. Hastily, she told Dr Anderson and her parents the story.

Dr Anderson acted at once and he and Uncle Quentin, George, Eric, and Timmy, were soon speeding back down the road to Devil's Point in his own car, much faster than George had dared to drive.

Of course, when they got there they found that Stein and his men had made off without further ado. But Victor was their main worry. He was lying on his bed, and he and Anne had managed to get a tourniquet round his arm – Victor had told the little girl what to do, and Anne's clever little fingers had followed his instructions. Dr Anderson immediately injected the anti-snakebite serum which would save Victor.

'He'll be much better in a day or so,' he assured the children. 'It was rash of you to drive that car, George, but you've saved Victor's life, and I'm going to ask Quentin to say no more to you about the risks you took!'

Anne hugged her cousin, and Julian and Dick thumped her on the back. They were all very glad that their alarming night had ended so well.

Things were more or less back to normal next morning. Victor had been taken to hospital, and was making a good recovery. It turned out that the damage to the laboratory building was not too bad. Once more, Dr Anderson congratulated the Five, who were pleased they had been useful.

'And this time,' said Eric, 'my father can lay an official complaint against Stein, thanks to you. There's your evidence, and Victor's, and we also have concrete proof in the form of the black car, and Stein's own jacket. Those three will soon be behind bars!'

But Eric was being over-optimistic. At lunchtime his father told them about the latest developments.

'I'm afraid we were counting our chickens before they'd hatched,' he said. 'The police haven't been able to arrest Stein and his two henchmen – none of them ever went home last night. All three seem to have disappeared mysteriously. My friend Dupont thinks they've probably left Martinique. It's certain that they didn't go by air, so they must have gone by boat. They've probably taken refuge on one of the neighbouring islands – St Lucia, or Dominica.'

'I feel so scared they'll do something else dreadful,' said poor Mrs Anderson. 'Stein is not a man to give up easily.'

But all seemed to be calm, for the time being at any rate. Uncle Quentin and Dr Anderson were very full of the scientific conference which they were both to attend. It was to open at St Pierre the day after next. Dr Anderson was going to talk to the scientists about his latest discoveries, and he was taking his precious formulae with him. Julian, Dick, George and Anne were delighted to be told that they could go with the two scientists. They would all be staying at a hotel in St Pierre, including Eric, and the Five would have a chance to see the town which had once been the capital of the island, until the volcanic eruption in 1902. 'I'll show you round the ruins,' Eric told them. 'There's an interesting museum there too. We'll start early in my car, and then we can take our time.'

So on the day of the conference they all set off – with the prospect of a pleasant day ahead of them. Dr Anderson took Uncle Quentin in his car, and the Five were in Eric's.

'The road is a very pretty one at this time of the morning,' Eric told them. 'And we'll have it almost to ourselves!'

He was quite right. George and her cousins admired the effect of the morning sunlight falling through the leaves of breadfruit trees, giant bamboos, and all the other vegetation of the tropical forest.

The two cars were going along in single file, with Dr Anderson's leading, when the peace of their surroundings was shattered. They had come to a particularly twisty place in the road, and Eric, going round a bend, had to break very suddenly so as to avoid running into his father's car. It too had just stopped all of a sudden.

'What's the matter?' asked Anne, alarmed.

One look was enough to tell her. There was a tree trunk lying across the road, and three men were standing on it, waving pistols at the two cars.

'Stein and his men!' said Julian.

The three wore big straw hats pulled well down over their eyes, and the voluminous clothes worn by cane-cutters. It was a very crude sort of disguise, obviously meant to take in anyone who knew nothing about them except the descriptions the police had circulated.

'Get out, all of you!' Stein said.

They had to obey. Stein went over to Dr Anderson. and snapped, 'Your briefcase, please!'

'Now listen —' the scientist began.

'It's too late to discuss it now. I want the formulae,' said Dr Stein, 'and I want them fast! Hand them over, or I fire at those children.'

'Better do as he says, Paul,' said Uncle Quentin. 'He doesn't seem to be joking.'

'Quite right,' said Dr Stein. 'I am not joking in the least!' And he put out a greedy hand for the briefcase Dr Anderson gave him, opened it, and glanced at its contents.

'Good! These papers are worth their weight in gold!' he said with great satisfaction.

White with fury, the two scientists saw Dr Stein's men get three bicycles out of the ditch where they had hidden them. There was nothing Uncle Quentin or Dr Anderson could do, because Stein was still waving his pistol at them. Then the three men jumped on the bicycles and rode off along one of the narrow paths which led deep into the forest.

'And we can't follow them in a car!' said Uncle Quentin angrily.

His friend was shattered. He kept repeating, 'My formulae! My precious formulae!'

Suddenly he heard peals of happy laughter behind him. Surprised, he turned to see the children laughing their heads off!

'Don't worry, sir!' cried Dick. 'Your formulae aren't lost!'

'I should say not!' agreed Anne. Her eyes were shining.

'Won't Stein be surprised when he sits down to read them!' said Julian, still laughing.

'Here they are, Father!' added Eric, giving his

father a piece of paper rolled up inside a news-paper.

'What on earth . . .?' stammered Dr Anderson. 'I don't understand.'

'Neither do I,' said Uncle Quentin. 'What does all this mean?'

'George got another of her ideas, that's all!' said Eric.

'Well, I only had to think what was likely to happen,' said George, modestly. 'We all helped to think of it, really.'

'And — and what *did* you think was likely to happen?' asked Dr Anderson, still wondering if he was awake or dreaming.

'Well,' said the clever girl, 'Julian thought Stein might still be on the island, and Dick said that if he was, he'd probably try getting hold of the formulae again. Anne guessed that the best moment for him to strike would be this morning, on this deserted road. So then *I* thought that the only way of avoiding any possible trouble was to swap the real formulae for some papers that didn't mean a thing.'

'George didn't want to tell you, Father, because you might have said it was all nonsense,' Eric explained. 'But I thought her idea was a great one, and I went and found some worthless old notes I'd once scribbled down, and put them in your brief-case instead of the formulae. And here *are* the formulae, safe and sound. Stein will be very surprised when he tries to figure out what the papers he's got mean!'

'Woof!' said Timmy, finishing the story.

The two scientists started laughing themselves, and then congratulated the children warmly. After that, they all set to work to move the tree out of the way, so that they could drive on to St Pierre.

It was still quite early when they reached the town, and the first thing Dr Anderson did was report the attack on them. He told the authorities that the three men wanted by the police were still on this island. Then they all went to the hotel where they were staying. Its manager was English, married to a Martinique lady, and their son Michael was a great friend of Eric's.

An hour after they had arrived, the two scientists left for the opening session of their conference, and the children went off to look round the town. They enjoyed their day's sightseeing with Eric and his friend Michael very much, and what with setting off so early in the morning, and all the excitement on the way, they were quite ready to go to bed after a good supper that evening.

Next morning, the two scientists had a very early breakfast before they left for their conference again. The children came down later, laughing and joking together.

'Hallo!' said Julian, entering the dining room. 'Eric's even lazier than we are! He isn't down yet either.'

'Well, I don't feel like waiting for him,' said Dick, looking greedily at the delicious tropical fruit waiting on their table. The four cousins sat down to enjoy their breakfast, and Timmy got a big bowlful of dog food, specially provided by Michael's mother.

'We must leave some fruit for Eric, though,' said George. 'He doesn't seem to be in much of a hurry this morning, does he?'

And when the children had finished their own breakfast, he still wasn't down. 'I'm going to see what he's up to!' said Dick, rising from the table.

'Let's all go,' said Julian. 'We'll jolly well get him out of bed!'

The four children ran up stairs and knocked at their friend's door. 'Come on, Eric!' they called. 'Get up, lazybones!'

But the young man didn't reply. Anne automatically put out a hand to the doorknob, and it opened. Julian put his head in.

'Time to get up, old fellow –' he began, and then he stopped dead, and went right into the room. Suspecting that something strange had happened, Dick, George and Anne followed. What they saw surprised them all. Or rather, what they *didn't* see – because the bedroom and bathroom were both empty. Eric's bed was neatly made up.

As the chambermaids didn't come to tidy the rooms until about noon, that could mean only one thing.

'He didn't go to bed at all last night,' said George, staggered.

'But he kept telling us how tired he was before we said goodnight,' Anne reminded the others.

'Something must have happened to him!' said Dick.

'And this must be the explanation,' said Julian, pointing to an envelope propped up on a table where it was bound to be seen.

The children read what it said, in large capital letters: 'URGENT – FOR THE ATTENTION OF DR ANDERSON.'

Timmy made a dash for the envelope and sniffed it all over, growling. 'Grrrrr!' he said, and the hairs on his neck bristled.

George went rather pale. She understood only too well what her dog was saying.

'Stein!' she said, horrified. 'I'm sure he's kidnapped Eric!'

Chapter Ten

WHERE IS ERIC?

'We'd better telephone Dr Anderson at the conference at once,' said Dick, and Julian made straight for the phone. Dr Anderson and Uncle Quentin were back very soon. George had guessed correctly – the letter really *was* from Stein. He had boldly kidnapped Eric the previous evening.

'I have your son,' he wrote to Dr Anderson. 'Don't force me to do anything violent! A young man's life is surely worth a few scientific formulae. You will soon receive my instructions concerning the exchange. Be sure not to tell the police, for if you do . . .'

'How dare he?' said the scientist furiously.

'Calm down, Paul,' Uncle Quentin told his friend. 'And whatever you do, don't let your wife know of this. We must look at every possible way of getting Eric freed ourselves.'

'I can see only one way,' said Dr Anderson

sadly. 'I'll have to let that villain have my for-mulae. He's put a gun to my head – and there's no other solution!'

That evening, a very small boy came into the hotel asking to see Dr Anderson. The boy handed him a letter, saying it had been given him by a man he met in the street – and the man had told him that Dr Anderson would give him some money in return!

Dr Anderson didn't feel like smiling at the audacious way in which Dr Stein had made sure his letter reached its destination without any risk to himself – he just tore it open, while Uncle Quentin gave the little boy a couple of coins. After all, it wasn't *his* fault! George and her cousins couldn't wait to hear what the letter said. Surely Dr Anderson was going to tell them? In fact, he had almost forgotten they were there! When he had read the letter, he told Uncle Quentin, in a low, toneless voice, 'If I want to see my son again alive, he says, I'm to go to the top of Mount Pelée at two in the afternoon on Friday – the day after tomorrow, that is. The place where I am to go is a spot where the crater has a cleft in it, and it is marked by a frangipani tree growing in a hori-zontal direction. I must go there to deliver my formulae alone. and then Eric will be handed over. Stein doesn't give any details . . . Quentin, I don't like this at all.'

Uncle Quentin tried to soothe his friend's fears.

The children tiptoed out of the room – they had been quite forgotten.

'Dr Anderson's hands are tied,' said Dick. 'He can't go to the police! Think of the risks he'd be running.'

'It's dreadful,' whispered Anne.

'Well, no sense weeping and wailing!' said Julian briskly. 'I think we'd better *do* something. Can't you come up with one of those great ideas of yours, George?'

'I only wish I could,' said George. 'The main thing is not to do anything silly – because that could endanger Eric.'

It was a gloomy evening. Uncle Quentin did his best to cheer his friend up, and managed to persuade him to go to the conference in the usual way next day, since there really wasn't anything else for him to do.

'It will be a way of passing the time until Friday, Paul,' he said. And Dr Anderson agreed. George was pleased.

'Well, that's something!' she told her cousins. 'At least we'll be free to do as we like all day tomorrow.'

'And just what are we going to do, then?' asked Dick.

'There's nothing to stop us going for a picnic on Mount Pelée, is there?' said George, in a meaning sort of voice. 'We're here to see the island of Martinique, aren't we?'

'We've already been up the mountain, though,' said Anne, puzzled.

But Julian sighed. 'I know what you're thinking of, George,' he said. 'You're forgetting one thing – we'd need a car to get to the start of that path up the volcano. It's quite a long way off. And we haven't any way of reaching it.'

'I'm not forgetting anything,' said George. 'I've already thought about a car – *and* a driver.'

'A driver?'

'Yes, of course,' said George. 'Michael! Eric's told him all about us and our adventures – I'm sure he'd be delighted to help!'

'Are you going to take him into our confidence?' asked Dick doubtfully.

'Why not? Nothing venture, nothing win! I like Michael, anyway, and he knows Mount Pelée inside out. I bet he'd act as our guide.'

The hotel manager's son, Michael, really was very nice, although the children had been too worried about Eric to take much notice of him. He was a tall, young man with brown hair, and they all liked what they knew of him – so it wasn't surprising that George had suddenly thought of him as a possible ally.

So the children went to Michael, asked him to promise not to breathe a word of the secret they were going to tell him to anyone else, and then told him the whole story. He gladly agreed to help them. 'It will be a pleasure,' he said. 'Of course I'll

110

go with you tomorrow – you can count on me!'

When Michael's little car drew up at the beginning of the path up the volcanic mountain next day, it was about nine in the morning, and the children still hadn't worked out a definite plan.

'This is mainly a sort of reconnaissance expedition,' said George, as they began to climb. 'But I do have a feeling that Stein must be hiding Eric up here somewhere. Probably in a place known to no-one but himself.'

'I expect his idea is to get hold of the formulae first, make off with them, and then write to Dr Anderson telling him where to find his son,' said Dick. 'That would be the best way for him to get safely away.'

'But why would he hide Eric near the meeting place, then?' said Anne. 'That would be a silly thing to do.'

'Or a very clever one,' said George. 'I bet Stein and his men are hiding out somewhere near the crater of the volcano – they're on the run from the police, remember. It would be safer and more convenient for them to have their prisoner actually with them. Of course, I may be wrong, but it wouldn't hurt to have a look around up there, would it?'

'No, it certainly wouldn't,' Michael agreed. 'You're tourists and I'm your guide – that's perfect cover! We'll see what we can find out.'

'And if we actually do discover anything – well, after that we'll have to play it by ear,' said Julian.

As they discussed their next moves, the Five and Michael were climbing the mountain path.

'I can take you straight to the place with the horizontal frangipani tree, if you like,' said Michael.

'I think it would be better if you just point it out when we're fairly close,' said George. 'Then two of us, no more, will go and take a closer look.'

'George is right,' Julian agreed. 'Just two scouts won't seem as obvious as a party of five.'

'Two people can probably get closer before being seen, as well,' said Anne.

'Actually, it would be best if they weren't seen at all,' said Dick. That is, if the kidnappers really are hiding out up there, of course. I suggest George and I do the scouting!'

'Right!' said George at once. 'And Timmy can come with us.'

They went on climbing, in silence. At last Michael stopped and pointed to a cleft in the outline of the crater's edge above them. 'There it is,' he said. 'See that rock fault? Well, the frangipani tree grows horizontally right across it.'

Chapter Eleven

STEIN IS CAUGHT

'Splendid,' said George. 'Coming, Dick?'

Julian and Anne stayed where they were with Michael, and George, Dick and Timmy went on through the lush vegetation which grew on the side of the mountain. Now and then mist hid the peak from their eyes. All was quiet around them.

Suddenly Dick stood quite still.

'Listen!' he said. 'There's someone coming!'

Looking up, George saw some bushes moving a little way ahead of them. And then two heads appeared, outlined against the sky.

'Oho!' said George. 'Monkey and Hercules!'

Sure enough, it was Simon and Felix, on the alert and inspecting the slope below them. The children kept perfectly still, hiding behind a huge flowering bush. But, unfortunately, a twig cracked as Dick moved his foot. The two men immediately looked their way. If they decided to go and see what was going on at that spot, they would find the children, recognise them – and the whole expedition would turn to disaster!

George could see only one way to distract the men's attention. She gave Timmy a little pat, and said, in a low voice, 'Tim – find Julian and Anne – quick! Find!'

And she pointed the way she wanted him to go. The intelligent dog looked at her. He couldn't understand why she was sending him away, but he was used to obeying his mistress, and when she repeated, 'Find!' he was off like a shot.

Of course he made quite a lot of noise as he ran. Leaves swayed as he brushed past them; pebbles rolled aside under his paws. The two men heard him, but all they actually saw was some kind of four-footed animal in flight.

'Stray dog,' said Felix to Simon.

'Or a mongoose,' said Simon.

Feeling that they now knew what the noises they had heard meant, Stein's bodyguards went away again. George breathed a sigh of relief. Her idea had saved herself and Dick from discovery. Once they were sure the men had gone, they hurried back, keeping as quiet as possible, to rejoin the others.

'At least we've found out one thing,' said George. 'The men *are* hiding out in the crater.'

When they got back to the hotel, the children and Michael held a council of war. By now all of them, including Michael, felt sure that Eric must be somewhere near the summit of Mount Pelée, along with his captors.

'And we must try to get him out,' said Julian. 'Look at it like this – if we fail, well, that's not too bad. We'll be in Stein's hands, and I'm sure he'll be glad to have more hostages, but that's all, and Eric's life won't be in danger any more. He'd never dare injure so many of us – and just think what a fuss Uncle Quentin would kick up. Stein's no fool, and he'd be sure to think of that. So this is where we've got quite an advantage over Dr Anderson, *and* the police. We can try something they're unable to do!'

This was good thinking on Julian's part, as all the children agreed – so did Michael, who insisted that he was going to be in the rescue party too. And so they drew up a plan of action, and began putting it into practice that very afternoon.

After Michael had driven them back to the volcano, the children spread out in a fan-shape as they climbed, making sure that they didn't lose sight of each other. They made their way slowly and cautiously up towards the crater.

But once they came within sight of the cleft in the rock, they all stopped short, and took cover. They had seen something alarming, if not entirely unexpected!

Stein and his bodyguards were just starting down a narrow path. They were walking at a leisurely pace, and passed so close to Michael that he could have reached out and touched them. However, of course he didn't – like the children he kept perfectly still in his hiding place behind a bush.

When the three men had gone some way downhill, the Five and Michael climbed much faster than before. The coast was clear, and they decided they'd better take advantage of that!

This time luck was on their side. They reached the rock fault, slightly out of breath, and leaned over to look inside the crater.

'There are caves all around the place here,' Michael told the children. 'Let's explore them.'

And they very soon found Eric! Poor fellow, he had been tied up and was lying on the ground. His eyes shone when he saw his rescuers, and he could hardly find words to thank them.

Once they had untied him, however, it turned out that he couldn't walk or even stand on his poor, numb legs.

'Never mind,' said his friend Michael comfortingly. 'I'm pretty hefty, and I'm sure I can carry you on my back, Eric. And if I get tired Julian and I will make a chair of our hands and carry you between us.'

It wasn't easy to hoist Eric up from the hole in the ground where he had been lying, and they had to take their time over it. Things got even worse on the way down the mountain – showers of rain come very suddenly on Martinique, and it began raining cats and dogs. And then, when the rain stopped, the children and the two young men saw Stein and his bodyguards on their way back. The three men recognised *them*, too!

'Oh dear – it's too late to hide! Whatever shall we do?' gasped poor little Anne.

Eric was very upset. 'It's all because of me you're in such trouble!' he said.

'But we aren't – not yet, anyway!' said Michael cheeringly. 'Look, here comes the mist. It may save us yet.'

Sure enough, thick mist was coming down, hiding the little party from their enemies. 'Come on, quick!' said Michael, making sure Eric was steady on his back. 'One of you must grab hold of Eric's shirt, and then the next must hold on to the one in front, and so on. Don't let go, whatever you do! Follow me, and don't worry. I'll guide you out of here – I know all these mountain paths inside out.'

So the children made their silent and slightly unsteady way back down to the plateau in single file, hanging on to each other. When they finally emerged from the mist, they saw Michael's car standing there, not far off, and they all rushed towards it.

'Good for that mist!' said Julian fervently. 'If it hadn't come down just then, I don't know *what* we would have done!'

'How on earth can I ever thank you all?' said

Eric, squashed into the car between Dick and Julian. 'I don't mind telling you, I was feeling awful down there in that cave, and I was furious with myself for letting those men kidnap me, just as if I were a baby! Did you know they were waiting in my room? They flung a blanket over my head and –'

'Don't let it bother you, Eric,' said Julian soothingly. 'Just think how glad your father will be to see you back safe and sound! He was desperately worried about you.'

It certainly was a wonderful surprise for Dr Anderson when Eric telephoned him at the conference to say he was back at the hotel, and there was a very touching meeting between father and son. It brought tears to the eyes of tender-hearted little Anne.

Dr Anderson really was delighted. 'Quentin, you have a most remarkable daughter!' he told his friend. 'And your nephews and niece are most remarkable too! Michael, you've done wonders as well. I don't know how to show you all my gratitude!'

There was quite a party at the hotel that night to celebrate the rescue of Eric. The young man had been able to tell the police many details of the place where he had been held prisoner, and they had gone straight off to surround the crater of the volcano.

'Surely they don't expect Dr Stein and his

friends to be sitting there waiting for them, do they?' said Dick incredulously.

He was right to laugh at the idea, for next morning Stein, Simon and Felix were still at large. Obviously, they would want to get out of the island as fast as they could, now that they were branded as kidnappers, besides being wanted for other crimes.

And perhaps they *would* have made their escape too, but for Timmy!

The children had said that while Uncle Quentin and Dr Anderson were attending the last day of the scientists' conference, they would like to go for an expedition to a fishing port on the north-east Atlantic coast of Martinique, which was said to be very picturesque. And they did enjoy their outing very much. Eric took his young friends to see the fishermen going out in their little boats on the rough waves of the Atlantic – they were wonderfully skilful at handling their small craft in those choppy waters.

'Except for those two!' said Anne suddenly, laughing. 'Just watch – they *do* look clumsy!'

And she pointed to two figures, one tall and the other short, who were trying to push a small fishing boat out to sea. There was another man in the boat too, and he was gesticulating wildly.

To everyone's surprise, Timmy suddenly started barking like mad. He took off and made straight as an arrow for the three men.

'Stein and his bodyguards!' cried George.

She and Timmy were quite right. Stein looked up, saw Eric and the children, uttered a cry of fury and raised his arm just in time to fend the dog off.

But Timmy was feeling determined, and he sank his teeth into Stein's arm. Howling with pain, Stein grabbed the dog by his collar and must have accidentally caught the buckle as he pulled because the next moment it had come away. He was left with the collar in his hands – and Timmy himself was free to attack again.

Seeing that their boss was in difficulties, Simon and Felix ran for their own lives instead of trying to help him. But as they were trying to get away, they collided with a number of the local fishermen, who were naturally curious to know what was going on, and had gathered round to look. The big man, Felix, thrust two of them violently aside – and that was his mistake. The other fishermen were horrified by his brutal behaviour, and flung themselves on him. There was a scuffle. Simon would have taken advantage of it to make his own getaway if possible – but the children and Eric weren't having any of that! They grabbed hold of him at once.

Eric made haste to tell the fishermen just what it was all about, speaking to them in their own Creole language. He soon had them all on his side. Before they knew it, Stein, Simon and Felix were surrounded, taken prisoner, and led off to the local police station near the little fishing port by a small but triumphant crowd.

Stein, who was seething with rage, was identified and imprisoned – at last – in a police cell along with his two bodyguards. The police from the capital, who had been looking for them in vain, would soon arrive to take charge of them. It turned out that Stein had had a simple plan – he had hired a fishing boat with an outboard motor, and intended to make for Dominica, where he thought he would be safe for a while.

He had reckoned without Timmy, however. The children were slightly stunned by the speed with which their pursuit of Dr Stein and his men had ended – it had looked as if it might go on forever, but then everything had happened so fast.

'It's all Timmy's doing,' George kept saying. 'Timmy is a really wonderful sleuth-hound!'

The local police of the fishing port were very proud of themselves, and telephoned the news to the police in St Pierre and Fort-de-France at once. Dr Anderson and Uncle Quentin were delighted to hear of it as they left the closing session of their conference.

'I can hardly believe it, Quentin, my dear fellow?' said Dr Anderson. 'Stein is in the hands of the police at last! Do you realise all that your visit to Martinique has meant to me? I was constantly tormented by that wretched man – I was almost afraid to work. I dared not be glad of my discoveries because I feared he would snatch them away from me! And then you and your wonderful family arrived like guardian angels!'

'Good gracious!' said Uncle Quentin. He couldn't help laughing. 'You're laying it on a bit thick, Paul, my dear fellow. I did nothing at all myself, you know – it was all due to the children!'

Dr Anderson turned to the Five.

'Eric and I will never be able to show you how grateful we are!' he said, sounding very emotional. The children felt a bit embarrassed, and wondered how they could make him shut up. But he went on, 'I only wish I could give you something that you'd like. Tell me what you want, and I'll do all I can to get it for you!'

George thought for a moment. 'I know!' she said, laughing. 'What we *really* want, Dr Anderson, is a new collar for Timmy! He lost his while we were having this adventure!'

And of course Timmy himself had the last word. Tail wagging furiously he let out a tremendous 'Woof!' The others just had to burst out laughing!

If you have enjoyed this book you may like to read some more exciting adventures from Knight Books. Here is a complete list of Enid Blyton's FAMOUS FIVE adventures:

WILLARD PRICE

A complete list of his thrilling animal adventures:

1. Amazon Adventure
2. South Sea Adventure
3. Underwater Adventure
4. Volcano Adventure
5. Whale Adventure
6. African Adventure
7. Elephant Adventure
8. Safari Adventure
9. Lion Adventure
10. Gorilla Adventure
11. Diving Adventure
12. Cannibal Adventure
13. Tiger Adventure
14. Arctic Adventure

Hal and Roger Hunt are sent all over the world by their father in search of rare animals with which to supply zoos. Their adventures on the way are full of action and suspense and every book is packed with information about the remoter regions of the earth, together with encyclopaedic facts about the world's animal kingdom.

KNIGHT BOOKS

WALTER FARLEY

THE BLACK STALLION ADVENTURES

The first time Alec Ramsay saw the Black Stallion he could hardly believe his eyes. The wildest of all wild creatures – beautiful, savage and splendid – was being brought onto the same ship which he himself was travelling on. The event was to change his whole life, for the strange understanding which was to grow between them would lead him through untold dangers to adventure in America.

KNIGHT BOOKS

CAPTAIN W. E. JOHNS

BIGGLES

Biggles and the Plot that Failed
Biggles Learns to Fly
Biggles Investigates
Biggles and the Dark Intruder
Biggles Sees too Much
Biggles Breaks the Silence

These gripping stories tell of Biggles, his friends and their dangerous flying adventures.

– NOW A MAJOR FILM

KNIGHT BOOKS